AF446894

SUPERNOVA

By Stephanie Hatfield

DORRANCE
PUBLISHING CO
EST. 1920
PITTSBURGH, PENNSYLVANIA 15238

The contents of this work, including, but not limited to, the accuracy of events, people, and places depicted; opinions expressed; permission to use previously published materials included; and any advice given or actions advocated are solely the responsibility of the author, who assumes all liability for said work and indemnifies the publisher against any claims stemming from publication of the work.

All Rights Reserved
Copyright © 2023 by Stephanie Hatfield

No part of this book may be reproduced or transmitted, downloaded, distributed, reverse engineered, or stored in or introduced into any information storage and retrieval system, in any form or by any means, including photocopying and recording, whether electronic or mechanical, now known or hereinafter invented without permission in writing from the publisher.

Dorrance Publishing Co
585 Alpha Drive
Suite 103
Pittsburgh, PA 15238
Visit our website at *www.dorrancebookstore.com*

ISBN: 979-8-88812-255-6
EISBN: 979-8-88812-755-1

PROLOGUE

Her dark hair blew in her face, sweat ran down her dark, freckled nose. She ran down the branch-riddled path, the gravel crunching beneath her feet, her armor clanking with every step. She was carrying two bundles of cloth. Inside the two bundles were the future of the universe, the only ones who could save our worlds, the ones who mattered more than anyone else as far as she was concerned.

Inside were the twin princesses of Elissium and Tartarus. Mirnova, the first born with a wild tuft of violet hair and large brown eyes, just like her father's. Then there was Nashmire, the second born. She had smooth white hair and her mother's icy blue eyes.

Mara ran through the forest to escape the wrath of the princesses' uncle, Draven Tarteren. He had gathered an army of thousands of demons and vampires and werewolves. All for the purpose of taking over and ruling both Elissium and Tartarus.

He wanted to use the power of the hybrid princesses to take over the kingdoms. So the queen sent her most trusted guard and told her to take the babies to Earth and hide them.

She was given strict instructions not to tell Queen Irene where the princesses were hidden just in case Draven gets to her and tries to force the information out of her.

No matter what, Draven cannot find these girls.

Mara took them each to a hidden location with a new family and prayed that the queen, the king, and their daughters would be reunited.

CHAPTER ONE

BEEP, BEEP, BEEP

I slap my phone off my bedside table and hear it fall to the floor.

"Ugggggh," I groan and roll over but end up rolling off the bed. I scream as I fall to the floor like my phone.

"Morning," my brother, Clark, says from the doorway, laughing his butt off. I flip him off from the floor and drag myself up.

"Morning, asshole," I reply.

"Alright, hurry up and get ready. You need to catch the train." I stand up, rubbing my eyes sleepily. I hate waking up in the morning. If I could stay in bed for the whole day, I would. I'm not depressed or anything, just a tired high school student. I drag myself to my closet and pick out an outfit. I pull on a checkered tank top, gray jean shorts and my giant gray cardigan. Perfect.

"SKY, BREAKFAST IS READY!" Clark yells from the kitchen.

"OKAY!"

I walk into the bathroom and brush my waist-length, naturally purple hair. Yes, my hair is naturally purple. No one can explain it. When I was a kid, I wore a blonde wig to hide the purple, but one day in middle school, I got tired of the blonde so I just didn't wear the wig anymore.

I flatten my blunt bangs and straighten my septum piercing. I walk out into the kitchen and plop down onto a chair.

"Here you go, kiddo," Clark says, handing me a plate of eggs.

"Call me 'Kiddo' again I'll kill you." He snickers. I devour the eggs.

"Okay, I gotta talk to you about something," Clark says, sitting down with his own plate of eggs.

"Okay, what's up?"

"Your birth mother reached out to me. She wants to meet you and explain some things."

"Is she going to explain my purple hair and the other weird things about me?"

"I hope so. So, are you up for it?" I slowly nod my head. Clark smiles and finishes his eggs.

"Alright, you gotta get to school." I nod and rise from my chair. Clark takes my plate. I walk over to the door and pull on my black platform creepers. They're only two inches tall, but I love them. I grab my backpack with little bat wings.

"See ya, Clark."

"See ya."

I walk out the door and head down the hallway. The elevator ride was slow cause everyone in the fucking building decided to use this elevator at the same time.

Once I finally escape the tenth circle of hell, I greet Chad, our doorman. He's a handsome, twenty-eight-year-old hunk of pure muscle. I like him. He sometimes sneaks me snacks from the vending machine.

The cool October wind hits me and blows my hair in a swirling tornado all around my face. The subway is busy, but I shove my way through the adults on their way to work and other students on their way to school. I hop on train 9 on the way to Sixty-Ninth Street.

I rise from the depths of NYC and follow the swarm of students walking into Thomas Jefferson High School.

One of the girls in perfect pleated skirts and matching blazers shoves me on the stairs. It was probably Jessica. Fuck Jessica. I don't support hating people, but Jessica makes that really hard. I nearly fall down the stairs but a steady hand grabs my waist and pulls me back on my feet.

"You alright there, love?" He has a beautiful soft voice that is smooth like butter and he has a British accent.

"Yeah. It's probably just Jessica and her friends." We continue into the building.

"Hey, do you by any chance know where Mr. Duke's class is?" he asks.

I look at him. "Yeah, I actually have his class first too. Follow me." I grab his arm. He is taller than me (Which isn't hard considering I'm 4'11".) He has messy, dirty blond hair, brown puppy-dog eyes, and a beautiful smile.

Okay I'll admit it; he's really cute. I really hope we become friends.

"So, what's your name?" he asks me.

"Oh, I'm Skylar, but most people just call me Sky. What's your name?"

"Olivar."

We make our way to Mr. Duke's class, making small talk and just trying to get to know each other. We finally arrive and Olivar takes a seat right next to me. Mr. Duke makes Olivar introduce himself in front of the whole class. If I had to do that I would cry. He sits back down and wipes his hands on his tan pants. Jessica glares daggers at me and dreamily looks at Olivar. Guess I'm not the only one to find him attractive. But he's paying attention to me. Most people in this school just ignore me and the rest are either my small group of friends or they bully me.

"Hey, Sky, do you want to sit with me at lunch?" Olivar asks.

"Sure, I'll introduce you to my friends. They'll love you." He smiles, his eyes squinting. "Alright, show me your schedule and let's get you to your next class."

CHAPTER TWO

Lunch couldn't come any slower. I meet up with my best friend, Lily, and introduce her to Olivar. She is excited to have a new student and is asking him a million questions. Lily will not stop talking as we move through the lunch line and when we go to sit down. She's much more extroverted than I am.

"So, have you been to the Uno Mas diner yet? My dad owns it," she says.

"Yeah, they make the best burgers in town," I cut in.

"I'll have to tell my parents about it." He smiles and takes a bite of his burger. His face twists in disgust. "Bloody hell, what is in that thing?" We all giggle until our friend Ari walks over with her tray.

"Sorry I'm late, Mrs. Smythe, that bitch, kept me late cause I forgot to do my homework last night."

I speak up. "Weren't you in a car accident last night? Oh, by the way, are you okay?" She nods.

"Yes, yes, I'm okay; no one was hurt, and I told her this and she said and I quote, 'That's no excuse. You need to be more responsible and tell your parents to drive better.' Like, what the hell. Oh, hello, you must be the new kid; I'm Ari." She reaches her hand over and Olivar takes it and shakes it.

Lunch ends too quickly and Olivar and I head to drawing class. We reach the classroom and I watch Olivar look in awe at the colorful, art-covered walls, Christmas lights hanging from the ceiling, and the comfy bean bag chairs inside.

"This place is beautiful." I giggle and walk over to my seat. He follows me and asks,
"Did you do any of the pieces on the wall?"

"Yeah, I did that one." I point to a painting of a sunset with a silhouette of a large tree.

"It's beautiful." I blush and smile.

"Thanks."

The teacher, Ms. Clay, walks in and smiles at everyone. Her eyes land on Olivar.

"Ah, we have a new pupil today. Welcome, sir." She curtsies and bows her head. Olivar bows his head back. Ms. Clay is a bit crazy, but she's really nice.

We all get started on our projects. I'm working on a hyper-realistic picture of an eyeball. Olivar starts on a portrait of someone in colored pencil. I smile at him and continue on my piece.

I help Olivar to his last class and basically run to my final class, choir. I love to sing. I walk in and take my seat next to Ari and this girl named Naomi. Naomi is really really nice.

Mr. Knight walks to the podium in the center of the room and taps his conductor's wand against the metal.

"Attention. Attention everyone. Focus on me please and thank you. Now let's get started." He raises the wand and we start warming up.

Around the middle of class, Mr. Knight has to take a phone call, so he leaves us alone. I am talking with Ari until I feel a hand grip my shoulder. Ivey spins me around so I'm facing her.

"You bitch. Hogging the new kid to yourself. Stay away from him or we'll make your life a living hell."

"You already do," I say under my breath.

"What was that freak?"

"Nothing." She scoffs and walks away.

Ari taps my shoulder. "Are you gonna stay away from Olivar?"

"No. I'm not scared of Ivey."

"Good cause I like hanging out with him." We laugh as Mr. Knight walks back in.

CHAPTER THREE

Olivar and I trade phone numbers before we leave school. I fight my way through the subway once again. I don't know why it's like all of NYC decided to take the subway at this exact time, but I just elbow my way through the wall of bodies to catch my train.

I catch it and make it back to the apartment without getting kidnapped. When I get there, I see Clark laying on the couch watching the news.

"Why are you watching the news, you nerd?" I poke him on the back of his head.

"I just like it. And who are you to call me a nerd?" I giggle and walk into my room awkwardly. I flop onto my bed and feel a vibration in my back pocket. I pull out my phone and see that Olivar texted me.

O: *Hey*

S: *Hey, what's up?*

O: *Nothing much. I'm just bored with homework.*

S: *I just got home, I haven't even started yet.*

O: *We should probably stop talking and get on with homework.*

S: *Yeah, I guess.*

O: *Okay, I'll talk to you later.*

S: *Later.*

I turn my phone off and flip over on my bed. I really hate homework, but I have to do it. I start with my math homework cause Clark always says, "Do the most difficult things first; then do the easy stuff." So math it is.

I finish all my homework and walk out into the living room.

"Hey, Clark, what's up?"

"Nothing much. Are you excited to meet your birth mother tomorrow?" My face goes red with nerves.

"I think so." Clark reaches over and rubs the back of my hand.

"It'll be okay."

I nod and smile. "Alright I'm getting in the shower." Clark nods and I walk into the bathroom. The shower water is steaming when I hop under the spray. The hot water soothes my tense muscles. I wash my hair and shave my legs.

Once I'm done in the shower, I go into my room, which feels like an igloo. I can feel the cold piercing my bones. That's a bit dramatic. I put on a big T-shirt and baggy sweatpants. Clark makes dinner and hands me a plate when I walk into the kitchen.

"What'd you make?" I ask.

"Pasta." I smile and sit down at our small table. I stuff the pasta into my face and put the dish in the sink once I'm done.

"I'm going to bed," I say to Clark. He nods and goes back to the news. I still think he's a bit of a nerd for enjoying the news. I crawl into bed and fall asleep once my head hits the pillow.

CHAPTER FOUR

I wake up but didn't fall off the bed this time. I grab my glasses off the bedside table. I walk to the bathroom to tame my mess of hair. After brushing my hair I go to get dressed. This is easily the hardest part of my day. I am a very indecisive person. I pull on a black T-shirt dress and my short gray and black cardigan.

(I also put on shorts so don't get any pervy ideas) I can smell the hashbrowns Clark is cooking. My mouth starts watering and my stomach growls. I walk out of my room and sit down at the table.

"Hashbrowns for you, my lady," Clark says with a flourish. He hands me my plate and bows dramatically.

"Okay, Mr. Drama Club. Good morning."

"Good morning.

I finish my breakfast and put my plate in the sink.

"Bye, nerd," I yell as I pull on my combat boots and grab my backpack.

"Bye, kid," he yells back. Luckily the elevator was not as bad as it was yesterday. Chad waves at me and I give him finger guns and head out to fight the subway once more.

I fight the crowd and make it to school in time, where I see Olivar standing there waiting for someone. He sees me and his face lights up. He speed walks over to me.

"Hey, do you want to walk to class together?" he asks.

"Sure." I smile. We walk together talking about anything and everything. We like a lot of the same things. When we walk into the classroom, I get death glares from Jessica and Ivey. We sit down and wait for class to start.

Lunch comes much quicker than yesterday and I meet everyone in the line. We sit at our usual table. Thank God today is popcorn chicken day. Popcorn chicken is the best thing these kitchens know how to make. Suddenly I feel a chill in the air. I turn in my seat and see Ivey standing there, a large cup of water in her hand.

"I thought we told you to stay away from Olivar." I stand up, I only reach about nose height on her.

"You don't scare me."

"You should be scared." She throws the water in my face. I look at her and calmly walk out of the commons. Ari and Lily follow me into the bathroom.

Ari grabs paper towels and dabs at my face.

"Are you okay?" Lily asks.

"Yeah, it's just water." I place my hand on her shoulder.

"Are you sure?" Lilly asks

"I'll be fine." They finish helping me.

"Let's get back to lunch," Ari says. We all nod and exit the bathroom. Olivar comes running over to us.

"Oh my God, are you okay, Sky?" he questions.

"Yeah, I'm fine. It's just water." He nods and exhales in relief. The bell rings and we head off to class.

CHAPTER FIVE

Class ends quickly and I head off to the subway to find the hotel where my birth mom is staying. The large Tucker Grand Hotel stands tall in front of me. I walk in and approach the front desk.

"Hello, I'm here to see my mother, Irene Elissite."

The lady looks me up and down and picks up the phone. "Hello, someone claiming to be Queen Irene's daughter. Can you send someone down?" My jaw almost hits the floor. My mom is *the* Queen Irene?

After a few minutes, two men dressed in suits come over to us, look me up and down, and say, "Come with us, miss."

They lead me to an elevator and usher me inside. They press the button for the penthouse floor and we shoot up. The doors open. Inside this room was marble flooring, tall pillars, plush furniture, and expensive china. I walk in slowly and see a beautiful woman with long, black hair and icy blue eyes.

She looks up and smiles at me. "Come in, come in, my dear. Oh look at how you've grown." She stands up and walks gracefully over to me.

"Mom?"

She pulls me into a tight, warm hug. "Yes, dear. Oh!" She cups my cheeks. "You have your father's eyes. Come sit, I have a story to tell you." I nod cautiously. I follow her over to the couch and sit down. "Now, I'm sure you want to know why I gave you up, right?" I nod. "Well, it's a long story. You are not an ordinary person. You are not just Skylar Nova Kent; you are Princess Mirnova Elenora Tarteren. You are a demon/angel hybrid. And future queen of Tartarus and Elissium. You were born in Elissium, think heaven, but when you were a baby your uncle attacked us to try and take over the universe. We had to hide you from Draven because he wanted to take you and your twin sister, so when he attacked, you were both sent to Earth. It took us a while to find you and we still haven't found your sister, but we're looking."

"Oh my God. Are you lying to me?"

She looks taken aback. "Why would I lie about this?"

"You know this does explain a lot."

"Yes, you have a lot of different powers and this—" She makes a book float over to us with her mind. "—will help you understand everything." She hands me the small leatherbound book.

"Thank you, my lady."

She waves her hand. "Oh don't call me that. Just call me Irene or you could call me Mom." She smiles a perfect smile, her teeth a blinding white.

"I'll try, Mom." I smile.

"Alright, you better get back home and start on your homework, but before you go, I have something for you." She reaches over to the grand coffee table and picks up a beautiful box with filigree on it.

"This is for you." I take it out of her hands and open it. Inside there is a gorgeous necklace. The necklace is a golden moon with sparkling diamonds embedded into it. I immediately take it out of the box and put it on.

"Thanks, my—I mean Mom." She cups my cheeks again and kisses my forehead.

"Now, get going and do your homework." I give her a thumbs-up and exit into the elevator.

Once I'm alone in the elevator I let out the biggest breath. I didn't even know I was holding my breath. I walk out of the elevator and head for the subway.

Clark is in the kitchen when I get home. Something smells heavenly.

"Mmm… what's for dinner? It smells so good."

Clark chuckles from the kitchen. "Pan fried chicken and potatoes." I put my bag by the door and sit at the table. He offers me a plate and I start eating.

"So, did it go well?"

"Yeah, I'm apparently a demon/angel hybrid. I got a book to help me understand my powers that I'm supposed to take everywhere."

"That's good." We continue to eat in silence. Once I'm done eating, I grab my homework and walk into my room. I flop onto my bed and start working.

CHAPTER SIX

Today already starts great (hint at the sarcasm). I get my long black skirt caught in the elevator door, I spill orange juice on my shirt so I have to change, and I almost miss my train. Olivar was waiting for me again to walk to class together.

In the middle of class, I ask to go to the bathroom. I bring my bag to make sure I have the book with me. I hope they think I need my bag for period reasons. Once I'm done in the bathroom, I feel the room get oddly cold. I notice ice beginning to form under the door.

"What the fuck?" I say out loud. The ice approaches me but stops six inches around me. I pull the book out and flip through the pages. On the page I land on, it says that my body temperature is in the 600-degree range. So that's why the ice melts before it touches me.

I gotta do something. I know. I could be a hero, but I need a disguise. I flip through the book and find a clothes changing spell. Perfect, this is what I need. I read the spell a few times and say it out loud. A cloud of purple smoke surrounds me.

I look in the mirror once the smoke clears. I'm standing there in a black spandex-like suit with a purple dress-like short-sleeved over-covering with a leather harness around my waist that attaches to a holster around my leg. Inside the holster is a retractable bo staff. I use the spell to summon a mask to protect my identity. My old combat boots transform into these thigh-high lace-up platform boots. My hair is pulled into a high ponytail on top of my head.

Everywhere I step the ice melts. I walk over to the door and try to open it. It doesn't budge. I place my hand on the door and try to focus all the heat in my body into my hand. It doesn't work. I focus harder, trying again to push my body heat towards my hand. Nothing happens. I don't know why. I grab the book and flip through it. I finally find the page that tells me how to work with my heat. I just need to say a small spell.

"*Valmore*"

I feel the ice begin to melt beneath my fingertips. Once it's melted enough I force the door open and walk into the hallway. I want to scream and giggle and jump up and down for joy. I can't believe that worked. The scene in the hallway was ripped straight out of frozen.

A shiver runs down my spine as I just notice the two holes in the back of my new outfit. *I must have wings,* I think. I pull out the book and flip through it once more. Yes! I do have wings. I just need to figure out how to grow or summon them. I look at the book and it says to touch my necklace to summon my wings. I do so, and feel the wings rip through the skin on my back. It doesn't hurt, though, just tickles as the feathers puffed out. My wings were large and black.

"Holy shit balls!" I whisper. A noise from the end of the hallway makes my head snap to attention. Icemen leading lines of students walking them somewhere. I hide as best as I can and sneakily follow them. The icemen lead the students to the gym. I peek through the doors and see Ivey standing in the middle of the gym, freezing people to the bleachers and looking through the crowds. Shit, she might be looking for me. I open my book and find a cloning spell and cast it on myself. I notice the clone is wearing what I'm currently wearing. I say the clothes spell on her and nothing happens.

This time *I* change back into my normal clothes. The icemen turn and look at the smoke that surrounds me. One of them turns towards my direction. I freeze, no pun intended, and try to hide behind the lockers.

I flip through the book and make a clone and shove her out. She looks around confused and screams as she sees the icemen approach her. They grab her and pay no attention to me. They march off with my clone in tow.

I wait for the icemen to leave before I change back. My wings itch a bit as I change back. The icemen walk towards the gym. I follow behind them and peek through the door. I see Ivey still standing in the center of the room, but now directing the icemen to take certain people to different places. Most of the students are in the bleachers with ice holding them still.

Ivey's hair is streaked with white and she has a huge staff in her hand. The staff has a crystal snowflake on top. I see her make eye contact with Olivar. She motions the icemen to bring him to her. "So, you wanna hang out with me and ignore Skylar now?" He looks terrified. This is my time to step in.

"Oi, freezing the whole school is no way to get a guy's attention," I say walking into the gym the ice melting with every step. Her head snaps towards me, her normal green eyes now glowing blue.

"Who the hell are you?" she snaps. I need to think of a name. Well, my name is Mirnova and that has Nova in it. And Supernova rolls of the tongue nicely. I think that's it.

"I'm Supernova." She giggles at my name, but I hold my head high and puff out my chest. "I'm gonna need you to thaw this place or I must warn you, I've taken a kickboxing class."

"What can you do against *me*?" She blows an ice blast at me. I try to stop it in its tracks with fire. Of course this doesn't work and I get hit right in the chest with ice. I feel it melt the moment it touches me. I wish I could pull out my book and find out how to stop her.

She throws another blast at me, but this time I feel a warmth within me rise up and I'm able to block it with a ball of fire forming within my hands. She looks shocked and pushes harder with her blast. I respond by pushing back. The flames grow stronger and light up my face in golden light.

"I said let everyone go."

"No." She lowers her hands and the blasts instantly stop.

"Fine. you leave me no choice." I land in front of her and pull out my bo staff. "Come at me, bitch," I say, motioning at her. She holds her staff defensively. I swing mine at her and smack her right in the stomach. She manages to whack me in the knee. I drop down to my other knee and hold my staff for balance. She seems to think about her next move. I thwack her right in the hip and hear her curse under her breath. She tries to freeze my feet to the floor but my body heat instantly melts the ice. She grunts in anger and moves to hit me again. She gets me in the side of the head and I start to hear ringing in my ear, but I'm still standing.

She's getting more angry the more I evade her efforts to beat me. She blasts me in the chest and I go flying across the gym, almost hitting a group of students and icemen. I stand back up and dust myself off.

"Why won't you quit, you pathetic little bitch?" Ivey cackles.

"Because I'm not one to quit once I start something." I swing again and Ivey slips on the melted ice and falls to the ground. She points her staff at me and tries to blast me again. This time I'm ready for it and dodge it. I slip behind the bleachers and pull my book out.

I flip through the pages and find one that tells me how to make a beam of energy shoot from my hands. I memorize how and hear Ivey's taunting voice.

"Come out, come out wherever you are."

I dart out from the bleachers, right into an icy ray. I form my beam of pure energy and it sprays out where our two blasts meet. I yell for the students closest to us to run away and get somewhere safe. I push my power forward and watch as my beam grows closer and closer to her. She tries to push back, but I'm too determined and strong for her to stop. My beam hits her in the chest and sends her sprawling across the floor knocking her out briefly. She stands up and throws her staff away. I copy her and prepare for a fistfight. She does seem a little dazed from the blow I gave her. She swings and she misses by a few inches. That blow must've really messed her up. I get her right in the jaw, sending her sprawling across the floor again.

The white in her hair retracks into her head, returning her hair to its usual red color. Everything starts to thaw. The students start to move out of their seats and walk towards me. I notice empty, open windows at the ceiling. I fly up to them, but I hear them all shout, "Wait, wait, who are you?"

I smile and say, "I'm Supernova." I fly off and land in an alleyway beside my apartment. I do the clothes spell again and the smoke surrounds me once more, and once it clears, I'm in my normal clothes.

I walk into my apartment to see Clark standing in the living room with the news on. The story of what happened at school, including some video someone took of me and Ivey fighting, was on the news.

"What did you do?" he asks.

"I was a hero. I saved my friends and the whole school."

"How did you get the disguise?"

"The book my mom gave me. It was a spell."

"Well, were you at least careful?" I nod. "Good."

"Does that mean I can still do it? I want to be a hero."

He thinks about it for a minute and says, "Yes, just be careful and be smart with who you choose to tell." I squeal in excitement and run to my room to do my homework.

CHAPTER SEVEN

I think I've gotten the hang of this whole flying thing. It takes some getting used to but is very fun. I land in the alley and magic my normal clothes back on. I'm so thankful no one follows me when I fly. I need to go do my art project. Thankfully I brought it home with me.

While working on my drawing, I FaceTime Olivar who is also working on his drawing project.

"If I have to look at another zoomed in pile of clothes for my value project I will stab my eyes out with an ice pick," he says in his beautiful accent.

"It's okay, you'll live." I roll my eyes at him.

"Hey, tomorrow do you want to meet up with me, Lily, and Ari at Uno Mas?" he asks.

"Sure, I'll ask my brother." I press mute and walk into the living room where Clark is writing his article for his job.

"Hey, Clark, is it okay if I go to Uno Mas tomorrow with Ari, Lily, and Olivar?" He seemed to think about it and turns to me,

"You still got that pepper spray I gave you?"

I nod but say, "You do know I'm a literal superhero. I can handle things myself."

"I know. Alright, sure you can go. Just be careful." I hug him and walk back to the table. I unmute the call and smile.

"I'll see you tomorrow."

"Awesome." We go back to working on our projects.

I wake up to my alarm instead of Clark waking me up. I rub the sleep from my eyes and head to the bathroom. My hair is not as big of a mess as it normally is so I don't have to spend as long brushing it. I pull it into two braids and fluff my bangs. I walk into my closet to pick out an outfit. I pick a flowy black dress with tortoise shell buttons down the front and a thick corduroy jacket. Perfect.

I walk out into the living room and pull on my combat boots. "Clark, where's my purse?"

He walks over and hands me my brown bag. "Have fun. Be careful."

I smile and nod. Twisting on my heel I throw my left foot forward and head out the door. I hate this fucking elevator. Why are there so many people? And so many stops. It takes us a good ten minutes to get to the first floor.

"Hey, Sky," Chad greets me from the front desk.

"Hey, Chad. What're you reading?"

"*Misery*."

'Nice, that's a good one."

"Yeah, it's really good so far."

"Alright, I better go and let you get back to reading. See ya."

"See ya later."

I nod and walk out the door. A chill runs down my spine when I step out into the cold.

The walk to Uno Mas was uneventful and nice. The sun made it feel a little less cold. Of course the cold didn't really affect me, with the whole "fire running through my veins" thing. Uno Mas is a short five-minute walk from my apartment. When I arrive, I see the group sitting at our usual booth in the corner. Ari stands up and hugs me.

"There you are, bitch."

"Hey, bitch." I slide in next to her just as Alice gets to our table.

"Ah, our favorite regulars. And a newcomer. What's your name, sweet pea?"

Olivar smiles his perfect smile and replies, "I'm Olivar Reed. It's a pleasure to meet you, miss—" He looks at her name tag. "—Alice." She smiles and takes our usual order. Ari gets blueberry pancakes with extra blueberries; Lily gets a loaded omelet with bacon on the side; I get a burger with lettuce, bacon, cheese, pickles, ketchup, and fries; and Olivar tries the classic scrambled eggs with bacon and hashbrowns.

We all get to talking and time seems to fly by. Our food arrives quickly and we all watch in excitement for Olivar's first bite of Uno Mas's incredible food. His face lights up once he puts the fork in his mouth.

"This is amazing," he says, bits of egg flying out of his mouth.

"Whoa, check this out," Lily says. She holds her phone up. Displayed on her screen is a news article that says. "Local NYC teens being taken off the streets."

"We should be careful," Lily says.

"Yeah, maybe we should go to someone's house that's closer," Ari says.

"My apartment is a five-minute walk from here and I have pepper spray," I say.

"Is it cool we go to your place instead of Olivar's?"

"Let me call my brother." I slide out of the booth and stand at the front of the diner.

The phone rings twice and then he picks up. "What's up, Sky?"

"Have you seen the news about the teens getting kidnapped?"

"No. What's been happening?"

"Teens have been getting kidnapped off the streets. So we don't wanna risk getting taken by walking the long way to Olivar's house. Do you think we could come to our place?"

"Yeah, just be careful." I squeal and thank him. He hangs up and I walk back up to my group.

"Clark said it was cool if you guys come over."

We finish our food and pay and tip. As we walk down the sidewalk, we notice it was getting dark outside. *How late were we out?* And this black van keeps following us. Suddenly four people jump out of the car and grab us. I start kicking and screaming and try to grab my pepper spray, but the can falls to the concrete and rolls into a storm drain.

"Nice try, Kitty," the man whispers in my ear. They cover my mouth and drag us into the van. Suddenly there's a gun against my head. Ha, like that'll do anything.

"All of you stay quiet or I blow her brains out." I close my eyes. I hope they think I'm scared of the gun.

Everyone goes deadly silent.

"Good job. Oh, you're quite the looker," the man holding Ari says, pulling her hair out of her face. Lily speaks up.

"My dad will give you however much money you want, just let us go," she says in a calm voice.

"Oh we're not holding you for ransom. We want you for a different reason," the masked thug says.

We sit in the van for a good twenty minutes. I try to track the turns we take, but we take so many it's hard to keep track. I can hear in his head that Olivar is trying to do the same thing. After those twenty minutes, we are pulled out into a giant warehouse. More teens line the walls of the warehouse. I feel the itch to turn into Supernova and save everyone, but that would reveal my secret to all my friends and that could be dangerous for them. They drag us over to a spot and chain us to a wall.

"My mother will find us," Ari snaps at the kidnappers. One of them grabs her by the hair and slams her face into the concrete floor. We see the blood drip out of her nose and down her chin, making little droplets on the floor.

"SPEAK WHEN SPOKEN TO!" the kidnapper yells.

CHAPTER EIGHT

By the morning Ari's nose was the size of a large orange. The bleeding has stopped pretty quickly so that's a good thing. I am able to set the bone after the initial pain has subsided.

"We gotta get her to a hospital. That was a hard hit she took," Olivar whispers in my ear.

"I know." Speak of the devil; Ari wakes up at that moment and lets out a loud groan.

I make up my mind. I don't care if my friends find out my secret. I have to save my friends and all these other teens. I turn to my friends. "Do not tell anyone who I am. If you do, I don't care if you're my friend, I will find you and hurt you. Spread the word that if anyone tells anyone else who I am, the same threat will happen to them." My friends look confused but begin to tell everyone quietly.

Once everyone has stopped talking, I grab the chains around my wrists and rip them off. My friends' jaws hit the floor. I whisper my spell and the purple smoke envelopes me. Everyone sits there stunned. The kidnappers finally regain their composure and rush towards me.

I pull out my staff and whack one right in the head. He's down for the count as another comes at me from behind. I sense it and let him roll off my back. I turn and slam my foot down on his back, hearing loud cracking sounds as I do so. Another man runs at me and gets me right in the knee. I drop to one knee and swing my staff until it connects with his face. I stand up and slam my elbow into the face of one other. My fist connects with a man's face and sends him sprawling across the floor. Suddenly a gunshot goes off. I feel the bullet rip through my forehead. I fall to the ground hearing My friends and the other kids start to scream.

After a few moments, I feel the bullet travel to my mouth and the hole in my head close. I stand up and spit the bullet out into my hand. "Good try, dude, but you're gonna have to do better to kill me." I throw the bullet right back at him. It rips right through his shoulder. He screams out in anguish.

The other men shoot at me a lot more times. I smirk and spit the bullets out. "You know, Einstein said, 'Doing the same thing over and over again expecting different results is the definition of insanity.' So why did you think that would work?" They look at each other, confused.

More men swarm around me and try coming at me more than one at a time. I flip one over my back and throw him into his buddy that was running up to me. They both fall to the floor in a heap.

"Alright, who's next?" I ask, waving my hand, motioning them towards me. Two more come at me. I grab them each by the shoulder and slam them into each other. They both fall down.

I have finally taken out all the kidnappers. I grab the keys and start going around and unlocking the chains.

"REMEMBER, DO NOT TELL ANYONE I'M SUPERNOVA. I DON'T WANT ANYONE I CARE ABOUT TO GET HURT BECAUSE OF IT!" I yell out as the teens run from the building. I turn to my friends who are just standing there, their mouths open wide in shock. I say my clothes spell and change back into my normal clothes. Ari is the first one to speak.

"Did that just happen? Did our best friend just reveal that she's a superhero?"

"Yes, that just happened. I am Supernova. I didn't want to tell you because knowing puts you in danger. You cannot tell anyone. I mean it." They all do the kid thing of air-zipping their lips, locking them, and throwing away the key.

"Okay. let's get out of here," Lily says.

We walk all the way back to the city. We got our phones back from the kidnappers and contacted our parents before our phones died. It takes us a good two hours to walk back. We meet up with our guardians at Uno Mas. Clark instantly envelopes me in a bear hug.

"I'm so glad you're okay. He leans down closer to me and whispers in my ear, "Did you transform in front of them?" I nod. "So they know?"

"Yes."

"Do you trust them enough?"

"Yes." He nods and releases me from the hug. I pull him back down to my level.

"I also threatened them that I would attack them if they told my secret."

"That works too." He smiles.

"Alright let's get you home." He grabs my shoulders and walks with me back to our apartment.

We walk in and I immediately head to the bathroom to take a shower. I make sure the water is nearly boiling hot, cause I can stand the heat, and hop under the spray. I wash away the events of yesterday and today. I wash away the ache in my head where I got shot. I wash away everything.

After a good twenty minutes, I get out of the shower and head to my room. The apartment is freezing. I start shivering and basically run to my room. I throw on an oversized, long-sleeved shirt, fleece pajama pants and fuzzy socks. The sheets smell fresh. Clark washed my sheets for me for when I get back. I climb under the comforter and fall into a restful sleep.

CHAPTER NINE

So things have been a little weird now that my friends know my secret. Whenever I'm on the news, beaten up after a particularly nasty fight, I get a barrage of texts and calls making sure I'm okay. It's nice to see them care. They also love to hear about my family and the search for my sister. We only ever talk about it in person or over the phone. We don't want anyone to find out my secret by looking at some text messages.

I wake up this Sunday morning to the sun streaming into my room. I roll over and put on my glasses. Looking at the time I realize Clark is already at work.

"Uggghhh!" I crawl out of bed and slump my way to the kitchen. I grab a bag of instant ramen and plop it in a bowl with water. I put it in the microwave. I wonder if my friends want to do something. I call them and ask. Olivar is the only one who isn't busy. I ask him if he would like to come over and hang out. Luckily Clark was gone and he doesn't care if I have friends over when he's at work. He says yes and that he'll be over in about twenty minutes.

I rush into my closet and try to pick out a cute outfit. I want to look good for him cause I maybe have a crush on Olivar. I throw on a black dress with a flowy skirt and a tan cardigan.

After a few minutes, I hear a knock at the door. I open the front door and see Olivar standing there in some tan pants and a light blue button-down. He also had a big, puffy coat in his arms.

"Come in, come in." I usher him in. He sits down on the couch.

"Those elevators are a nightmare," he says. I join him and grab the remote.

The news channel came on once the TV springs to life. Suddenly an emergency warning goes off and the news channel blares BREAKING NEWS. The female anchor looks dead into the camera and says, "We are getting reports of a spider woman attacking downtown. She is dangerous. Stay in your homes and do not leave." I look over at him.

"Go. I'll wait here where it's safe." I nod and change into Supernova. I climb out the window and fly downtown. All of downtown was covered in white, sticky strings of web. I have to be careful where I land. I blast some fire and burn the web and land on the ground. Standing on the web was a giant woman with the top half of a woman and the bottom half of a spider.

"YOU DARE BURN MY HOME!" she yells at me.

"This isn't your home. This is New York City. And You're trespassing. So I suggest you leave." She roars a mighty roar and rushes towards me. I dodge her attack and thwack her in one of her legs. She slides across the concrete. I let fire collect in my hand. I throw a fireball at her and just miss her. The web catches fire almost immediately.

"NOOO!" She yells out. Her eyes go red and she charges me with twice as much force. I take the brunt force of her attack with my arms. I grab her by the shoulders and throw her to the ground. She tries to stab me with one of her sharp legs but just barely misses my side. The next time she goes to stab me she succeeds. I grunt and hold my side seeing the thick black blood ooze out of my hip.

I blast more fire at the spider lady and it hits more of her web. She screams louder and it seems like she's in pain when I destroy the web.

"I'll give you one more chance; leave here, or I'll make you leave." She stares me down.

"Well, are you going to leave?" She just roars again. I blast her with a fire beam. She flies backwards and crashes through her thick webbing.

I then focus my fire on the web surrounding us. I walk over to the thickest part of her web and hold my hand over it. My side is still oozing blood down my side.

"LEAVE NOW OR I BURN IT!"

"NO, NO, FINE! I'll leave. I'll leave." She runs off in one direction.

I take the time to burn every piece of web in every nook and cranny of this city 'til there's none left. I could almost hear her screams as I did it. Once that's done, I fly back to my apartment and climb through the window. Olivar is there waiting and he sees the wound on my side.

"Are you okay?"

"Yeah, I'll be fine."

"It looks like it needs stitches. Should we take you to the doctor?"

"No, like I said, I'll be fine." I wobble slightly. I know the wound will heal quickly in a day or two but if I don't get it stitched up, it will heal with a giant scar.

"Do you know how to sew?" I ask Olivar.

"Yeah, why? Oh, you want me to stitch up your side." I nod and wince. I change back into my normal clothes and slowly walk to the linen closet. Olivar rushes over to me and helps me grab the sewing kit and leads me to the couch. He softly lifts off the side of my shirt and dabs some of the disinfectant he grabbed without me noticing. I wince slightly as it stings.

"You can take a bullet to the head, but you can't heal a cut on your side?"

"It'll heal quickly in a day." He smiles at me and threads the needle.

"Alright this is going to hurt. Wait here. I'll be right back." He stands up and walks back to the closet. He comes back with a small washcloth.

"Bite down on this. It might make it more bearable." I nod and stick the washcloth in my mouth.

He takes the needle and pushes it through the first part of my skin. I nearly scream and bite down so hard as he slowly sews my side back together. Tears stream down my face and evaporate into steam the second they touch my skin.

The whole thing takes no longer than ten minutes, but it feels like hours. Once he's done he puts a gauze bandage over it and pulls my shirt down.

"Alright, we're done."

"Good. That hurt so bad."

"I bet. Now I should probably get going. So, I'll see you at school."

"See ya." He stands up and walks to the door. Before he leaves he turns back and smiles at me. I smile back and he leaves.

CHAPTER TEN

So, I think I'm gonna tell Olivar how I feel about him. I hope he feels the same way. God that was so sappy. I climb out of bed on this rainy Saturday and shiver. It's freezing in here. I walk to my closet and change into some plush sweatpants and a baggie hoodie. I hug myself to try and warm up. Clark is off on a business trip, so I have the apartment to myself. I walk into the living room and turn up the thermostat. The hot air blows out of the vents and I sigh in relief.

After making a plate of eggs, I turn on the TV. It's still on the news channel. I turn on *Kitchen Nightmares* and relax into the couch. The eggs I made were good but not as good as Clark's.

Suddenly there's a breaking news message flashing across the screen. The news show flips onto my TV and shows helicopter footage of a person in black robes holding a large black stone with purple and gold swirls moving within it. The person is shouting.

"I AM THE DEMENTOR! YOU CAN'T HURT ME!" they yell at the cops approaching them. Surrounding them were bodies. They were breathing, but they were asleep or something. Then I noticed one body. It's Olivar. I instantly set down my plate and run to the window. I turn into Supernova and fly to where this person is.

I land in the field of sleeping bodies. I walk up to the cops, who have formed a barrier between the dementor and everyone else. They notice me and let me pass. I'm lucky that the cops like me (though I don't always like them). I walk up to the Demented.

"What did you do to all these people?" I ask calmly, approaching him.

"I stole their spirits!" he says in a sing-song voice. "And they're mine forever!"

I pull out my staff and hold it in an attack stance. "Give these people their spirits back, NOW!"

He smiles a sickening grin. "No." And poofs off in smoke.

Once he's gone, the police let the loved ones of the victims come and collect their sleeping loved ones. I turn back into Sky and help take Olivar back to my apartment. (He told me his parents were out of town as well. Some funeral.) Once no one can see, I pick up Olivar bridal style and take him to my room. I put him in my bed and pull the covers over him. He looks so peaceful. I push a lock of his hair out of his face and sigh.

I'm gonna need help to find this "Dementor" and get what this stone was that he had. I bet my mom might know what this is. I grab the book she gave me off my desk. I flip through the pages, trying to find a way to contact my mom.

"Yes, finally," I exclaim. It says to recite this spell while thinking of the person I wish to contact. I memorize how to pronounce the spell and once I'm confident, I say, *"Undo moray no gest."*

A shimmering form of my mom appears in my room.

"Hi, Mom. I need your help."

"What's wrong, Moondrop?'"

"Moondrop?"

"It's what I called you as a baby. Your sister was sunray and you were moondrop."

"Okay, anyway. This man stole a bunch of people's spirits with this black, purple, and gold swirling stone."

She seems to think, then exclaims, "He has a spirit stone."

"Wow, really creative name." I roll my eyes.

"Don't sass me, young lady."

"Sorry, Mom."

"If you break that stone it will release all the spirits. You have to break it quickly. These stones in the wrong hands could be really bad. Please get it back and break it. One less spirit stone in the universe is a good thing. Alright, good luck, Moondrop."

"Thank you, Mom."

She cuts the magic link between us. I sigh and sit down on my bed next to Olivar.

I need help finding this guy. I call Ari and Lily. Luckily Lily always has good ideas in sticky situations. I trust these two. They're smart enough to help me. They arrive within ten minutes. I usher them into my room.

"Whoa, you weren't kidding."

"Why would I be lying about this?" I question.

"I don't know. I'm sorry."

"It's fine, I just need your help finding this 'Dementor' guy."

We all sit on the floor and brainstorm.

"Do you have any kind of tracking spell in your little book?" That's a good idea. I told you Lily is good. I grab the book and flip through the pages.

"Yes! Found it." I open the book all the way and read the spell.

"Oh no, I need something that belonged to him to do the spell."

"I saw on the news the police picking up a piece of his cloak," Ari says.

"I'll head to the police station." I change into my supersuit and fly out the window.

It is hard finding the police station from above the city, but eventually I find it. I hide my wings and walk in. I walk up to the front desk and ask about the piece of cloth found at the scene. She makes a phone call and a man leads me into a separate room.

"Why do you need this evidence?" he asks me.

"I'm going to perform a locating spell, but I need something that belongs to the person I wish to find. In this case, that's the Dementor, so I need that piece of his cloak."

He seems to think. "The boss is gonna kill me for this, but if giving you this will help us get this villain off the street, I'll do it. You can have it. Just don't tell anyone.

"My lips are sealed." He leaves the room for about five minutes. He comes back with a plastic bag with the cloth inside.

"Now go. Save our city."

"Always will." I salute him and walk out of the station.

I fly back to my apartment as quick as possible. Luckily, it was cloudy so I could fly above the cloud line and not hit anything. I climb in through the window and change into my normal clothes.

"I got it." They all look relieved.

"Alright let's get cracking on this spell," Ari says, clapping her hands together. I sit on the floor with the rest of them and read the spell.

"*Almorn shac rents mees lar vore.*" The cloth starts levitating. It flies towards the windows and *thunks* against it. I turn into Supernova for the third time today and open the window. The cloth flies out the window and I follow it.

The cloth twists and turns through the skyscrapers and tall buildings. The cloth finally dips down into a window of a building. I climb through the same window and follow it into the basement. I hear through the door a masculine voice practicing evil phrases.

I kick the door in to find the Dementor standing in front of a mirror, practicing how to be evil. He turns around in shock.

"How dare you break the door to my evil lair." I nearly die of laughter at his cliché wording.

"Dude, talking like that does not make you scary. " He looks taken aback. "Now, you need to give me the spirit stone or things might get ugly." I hold my hand out. He spits at me. I grab my staff and swing it at him. He cowers in the corner.

"Fine, fine, take it, just don't hurt me." He holds out the stone. I take it and smash it. A bunch of tiny, glowing orbs fly out of the broken stone and return to the people they belong to.

"You really are pathetic. Turn yourself in to the cops or I'll take you myself." He nods and rushes out the door. I fly back home and see all my friends sitting on my bed.

"Morning, Olivar. You feel okay?" He nods and thanks me for saving him again. I smile and he leans in and kisses me. Lily and Ari look shocked. Ari starts clapping. I pull away and smile.

That might've been the best moment of my life. It was my first kiss.

"That was amazing," he whispers.

"You guys are so cute together!" Lily squeals. We smile and he hugs me.

"Ari, Lily, could we have some privacy?" They nod and leave the room. Olivar grabs my hands and kisses them.

"Skylar, will you be my girlfriend?"

"Yes, yes!" I tackle hug him and land on top of him on the bed. I kiss him again and feel butterflies swarm in my stomach. We pull apart and go and join Ari and Lily in the living room.

"Hey, do you guys just want to stay over? Don't worry about clothes, I can make you some." Ari and Lily call their parents. Their parents say yes so I use a spell to make everyone comfy pj's.

CHAPTER ELEVEN

Olivar and I have been dating for about four months now and we cannot get enough of each other. We love hanging out and talking on the phone and sitting with each other at lunch and the classes we share. Ms. Clay even lets us share one of her giant beanbags. Ivey and Jessica would glare at us anytime we kiss or he puts his arm around me, or when we just talk to each other. I just ignore them and focus on Olivar.

Olivar and I were on FaceTime just talking about random stuff when I get an alert on my phone. "DANGEROUS MAN ATTACKING EVERYONE UPTOWN." I tell Olivar about this and he tells me to go and save the city. I nod and hang up. I transform and fly uptown.

The scene there is a man who is about four foot thre trashing all the stands and glass around him.

"Oi, what the hell are you doing?" His head shoots in my direction. "I'M TIRED OF PEOPLE CALLING ME WEAK. I AM NOT WEAK! I will show them. I will show them all."

"I didn't call you weak. You clearly aren't."

"IT'S NOT YOU. IT'S EVERYONE ELSE IN THIS STUPID CITY!" Okay, this guy has lost it.

"Okay, just calm down. Let's talk this out like adults."

I'M TIRED OF TALKING THINGS OUT!" He rushes me. I take the brute force of his hit with my arms, holding him by the elbows. I throw him to the ground, but he pulls me down with him. He lands on top of me and starts punching me. I feel blood drip down my face as I fight to get him off of me.

I finally get him off me and roll on top of him. He thrashes his legs around beneath me, but I keep my hold. He escapes and goes to hit me again. He gets me right in the shin. I feel my bone snap in two and fall to the ground. I push my bone back in place and nearly scream in pain. I know this will heal in a day, but I have to stop this man. I struggle to stand up and slowly limp over to him. He smirks as he sees me limping. He comes rushing at me and I manage to get on top of him again.

I use a spell to summon strength resistant handcuffs and snap them on him. I stand up and let the police collect him. That might've been the quickest fight I've ever fought. I fly back home and collapse on my bed. My leg is throbbing and swollen. I change carefully and sit in bed for a while with and ice pack on my leg. I could barely walk, but I know it will be healed in the morning.

Olivar calls me and asks if I'm okay and I tell him about my broken leg but also say that it will heal by tomorrow morning. He lets out a relieved sigh and we talk until I get too tired to talk anymore.

I hang up on Olivar, turn off my lights, and fall asleep.

CHAPTER TWELVE

Clark decides we should take a trip to the beach. We never seem to hang out just him and me. I am of course all about it. I love the beach. I change into a black bikini with suns and moons all over it. I also put on some jean shorts so I'm not walking around the streets in just a bikini.

I walk into the living room and see Clark standing there with a bag and a few towels under his arm. I smile as he asks me if I'm ready to go. I nod and we head out.

Chad barely notices us. He's too engrossed with his book. It was quite warm outside. Not warm enough for me, but a literal fire is the only thing that will be warm enough for me.

The walk to the beach is quite nice. I enjoy the scenery and bask in the sunlight. Once we make it there, we set up our spot along with dozens of other beachgoers. I decide to go and hang out on the large secluded rocks off to the side. It was beautiful. No one else was there, thankfully. I like to be alone. The sun was glittering high in the sky, casting shadows on the rocks I was sitting on.

At that moment I heard a cry. I look around to see if someone was drowning or got stung by a jellyfish, or something like that. But I don't see anything or anyone.

Once again there is another cry. It sounds like it's coming from the water down by the rocks. I slowly stand up and tiptoe my way down the smooth stone.

I am in shock at what I see once I make it to the water's edge. I see a woman… well, she isn't quite a woman. Her olive face and arms are covered in glittering black scales that seems to sparkle with rainbows in the sun. Her hair is long and black and tangled with seaweed. Her inhuman blue eyes seem to pierce my soul.

She reaches up to me and speaks in Elissiate. "Please help me."

"What's wrong?" I ask. She pulls herself more up on the rock and exposes a long shimmering tail. She's a mermaid. My mom told me about them. They are peaceful.

Tangled around her tail is a thick green net. I reach out to pull the net off and she flinches away.

"I'm not going to hurt you. I want to help you. My name is Mirnova. What's yours?"

"Your Highness! My name is Tasi. Help me please!" I reach down and start to try and untangle the net from her tail.

"How did you get this way?"

"Humans can be evil and blinded by the thought of wealth from anything."

"You're not wrong."

"Will you help me with something else, Your Highness?"

"Yes, what's wrong?"

"My brother Haf was taken by humans and I need help from someone who can walk on land to get him back."

"Did you see where they took him?"

"No, they sailed away into the fog and I lost them."

"Bring something of his to me and I can use a locating spell to find him and bring him here."

"On it. I'll be right back." She dives under the water and I wait. She finally resurfaces and hands me a small clam.

"Alright, I'll be right back." She nods and laces her webbed fingers together. I cast the spell and watch the clam float in the air for a few seconds then zoom off into the city. I fly after it after transforming.

It stops in front of a large, gray, concrete building. It keeps tapping the door wanting to get in and reunite with Haf. I pry the door open and the clam dashes off down twisting hallways. I take off after it and see it stop in front of a door. I remove the spell and quietly open the door.

Inside there is a vat of water with a small boy with a long black tail, shiny scales, and messy black hair. There are three scientists standing above the merboy and writing things down as he swims around his small prison. I slowly walk up and knock out one of the scientists.

The other two look scared and throw their clipboards at me. They bounce off my chest and they just stand there. I punch one of them and kick the other in the stomach. They're both down for the count.

I run over to the merboy and pick him up out of the water and start running as fast as I can. It takes us, at most, three minutes to get back to the beach. I am pushing myself so fast. Tasi looks up at me standing over her as my shadow darkens her already dark form. Her face lights up when she sees me holding her brother.

"You did it! You found him! Oh, thank you so much, Your Highness."

"No thanks necessary, I just want to help my people. Now take your brother home and get him some food. His stomach was growling the whole way here."

She nods and gently takes the boy from my arms and places him in the water. He slowly opens his eyes and smiles when he sees our faces.

"What happened?" he asks.

"You were captured by humans, but Princess Mirnova saved you. You're safe now." He turns to me and bows his head the sunlight reflecting off his glistening scales. I bow back and start to walk away back towards Clark to tell him what just happened.

CHAPTER THIRTEEN

Summer went by quickly and it was time for junior year. Olivar and I are still dating and Ari got a boyfriend over the break. His name is Reed Smith. I've met him a few times. He is about five foot nine with fluffy dark hair and deep brown eyes. I read his mind and he truly cares about and is in love with Ari. Lily has just become our fifth wheel. We still love her.

I wake up and pick out an outfit. I pull on a black-and-white checkered skirt and a large long-sleeved shirt. Clark's out of town again, so I go and make myself breakfast again. I turn on the news (Yes, I'm a nerd like that now) and see breaking news. Atop a building is a gang holding Olivar off the edge of the roof.

I immediately jump up and rush to the window. I pry it open and fly out. The building was not hard to find with all the police lights and such. I land on the roof opposite the men.

"Bring him back from the edge," I growl out.

"Not until we get our money. You better stay there Dying Star or I'll drop him."

"No, don't do that. I'll stay right here." He nods and the man holding Olivar nods and lets go. I scream and rush forward, jumping off the roof myself. But I wasn't fast enough. I see his body explode down on the concrete. I fly to a close alleyway and transform into my normal clothes. I rush back to the scene and feel the tears fall in a steady rhythm. Olivar's parents are there wailing next to his body.

Suddenly my phone rings.

"Hello?" I answer, my voice shaky and raw.

"Is it true? What we saw on the news?" Ari asks me.

I choke back a sob and reply, "Yes. I'm sorry. I tried to save him. I tried. I wasn't fast enough."

"Skylar, it's not your fault."

"I can't be a hero anymore. I failed. That's it; Supernova has retired."

"Don't say that. It was an accident. You can still help people."

"I can't even protect my own boyfriend, let alone random civilians. No, I've made up my mind. I'm done." I hang up the phone and walk home in the pouring rain. My hair is sticking to my back and face once I arrive back at the apartment. Chad looks at me sympathetically.

"Hey, I heard about your boyfriend, Sky. I'm so sorry."

"I'll be okay. Eventually, I'll be okay." He nods and lets me go up to our apartment.

I walk in the front door and see Clark sitting on the couch watching the news. He immediately stands up and embraces me in a bear hug. I cry in his arms for a solid five minutes. He pulls away and says, "Ari called and said you quit being a superhero. Is this true?" I nod. "Well, it's up to you."

"Thanks." I pull him back into a hug.

The funeral was five days later, a Saturday. I put on a simple black dress and black kitten heels. I really didn't want to go. I don't like people seeing me cry. But Clark convinced me to go, so I did. It was stuffy in the small church where the ceremony was held. I got in line to see the casket. I felt a lump form in my throat get bigger and bigger the closer I got to him.

Finally, it was my turn. I look down at him. His hair was perfectly styled and he wore a pressed suit, blue button-down shirt, and black tie. I choke back my tears as I lean over and kiss him one last time. After my turn, I walk to my seat and sit down next to Clark. A single tear falls down my cheek and sizzles.

The funeral is miserable. And so is the coffin burying. I do what I am supposed to do. I drop my handful of dirt and read some speech I don't really remember writing as the past five days have been a blur. Clark finally lets us leave.

We walk back home and I immediately take a shower and change into pj's. I collapse into bed and cry myself to sleep.

CHAPTER FOURTEEN

The past few months have been a blur of going to school and hanging out with friends to try and distract myself from the pain I was going through and lying in bed wishing for this all to be some bad dream. I head to English class and run face-first into another person. I fall to the ground and drop all my books. Standing above me is a lean, muscular boy with fluffy brown hair with golden highlights that sparkle in the fluorescent lights. He has thin, wire-framed glasses and sharp golden eyes. I push my black thick frame glasses up on my nose.

"I am so sorry. I did not see you there, miss," he says in a voice that is low and smokey and sexy as fuck. He bends down and helps me up. He also helps me pick up my books.

"Um, do you know where Mrs. Montgomery's room might be located?" He's new here. I immediately remember Olivar and nearly start crying. But I gain my composure and smile at him.

"Yeah, I'm headed to her class as well. Follow me." He smiles a blinding white smile and follows after me.

"So what's your name?" I ask him.

"Felix Gifford. And you?"

"Skylar Kent, but most people call me Sky."

"That is a beautiful name." I blush and hold my cheek.

"Thanks."

We reach the door and he politely opens it for me.

"Thank you, kind sir." He bows his head at me and I bow back. I walk in and take a seat at my desk. Felix walks in and Mrs. Montgomery lets him choose where to sit and he sits next to me. We start reading *Wuthering Heights*. Felix seems to already know the book.

"Have you read this book before?"

He turns to me. "Yes, I have."

I nod and go back to listening to the teacher. I help Felix find his classes and we have a lot of classes together. He sits with Ari, Reed, Lily, and me at lunch. I hear Ari's thinking how similar this situation is to when we first met Olivar. I tell her in her mind.

"I know it's really similar, but I wasn't gonna leave him stranded on his first day. He needs friends and I am okay with being that friend."

"Okay just don't think of this guy as just a replacement for Olivar."

"I won't."

Suddenly I snap back to attention with Lily waving her hand in my face.

"Did you hear Felix?"

"No, sorry, I was a little distracted. What did you say?"

"I asked what kind of music genre do you partake in the most."

"Oh anything but country." He nods and gets up to throw away his lunch.

"Sorry, I often do not eat lunch. I have big breakfasts." We all nod in understanding. He throws his tray away and sits back down at our table. We talk until the bell rings and Felix and I head to History.

In History, Felix answers most of the questions as if he were there. I just noticed how pale he is. *Is Felix a vampire? No, that's crazy. But he didn't eat. But he said he had a big breakfast. He also talks kinda funny like he's from a different time.*

We exchange phone numbers and I head back to my apartment. Clark is home when I get there. He's in the kitchen cooking something.

"Oooo, what's for dinner?" I ask.

"Spaghetti and meatballs."

"Nice." He smiles at me.

"You seem to be in a better mood."

"Yup, I made a new friend. His name is Felix and he might be a vampire."

Clark drops the spoon he was using to stir the sauce. "He might be a what now?"

"A vampire."

"YOU MADE FRIENDS WITH A POSSIBLE VAMPIRE!?!?" I flinch at his volume

"Well, I didn't know he might be a vampire when I made friends with him."

Clark rolls his eyes and fixes me a plate. I devour it and go off to do my homework. I start with math. I fucking hate math, but I still have to do it no matter how much I hate it. Once I'm done I get into pj's and go to bed.

43

CHAPTER FIFTEEN

I wake up feeling oddly happy. I pick out an outfit. I put on a mesh top with embroidered stars on it, a black flowy, tank-top dress, and a belt with stars on it. Perfect. I walk into the bathroom and braid my hair into a braid crown. Alright I look good. Just need to grab my glasses. I pluck them off my bedside table and place them on my face.

I eat the breakfast Clark gives me. After food I grab my backpack, slide into my combat boots and leave for school. The elevator still sucks ass, but I've gotten used to it. I wave at Chad and run to catch my train. Some man elbowed me in the ribs cause I was apparently "in his way," but I ignore him and hop onto my train.

The train ride was uneventful and I exited as quickly as I could. Standing there was Ol—no it was Felix. He was waiting for me. I walk up and try to force Olivar away from my thoughts. I smile and let him walk me to class arm in arm like a woman being escorted to a ball. We arrive and he opens the door for me again.

"My lady." I curtsy and walk in and over to my seat. He joins me after holding the door open for a few other people.

"You're so nice to people. How do they not get on your nerves?"

"If someone is bothering me I just hit the mute button in my head and it is like they're not saying anything."

"You have to teach me how to do that. I would love to just mute Ivey and Jessica."

"Okay." Mrs. Montgomery walks in at that moment and tells us to get out our books.

Class went by fast and Felix didn't eat anything at lunch again. We were in math class when I notice a sudden chill in the air. Oh no, someone really pissed off Ivey. I ask to go to the bathroom. Mrs. Rinley says yes. I see the ice cover the floor and a ring of melted ice around me. I'm the only one who could stop this. But what if I can't do it. What if I fail again. I feel my hands shake and feel the fire flowing through my veins. The ice around me starts to melt farther away from me. Fine, I'll do it. I'll be a hero. Again. This is gonna be so hard.

I whisper my spell and turn into Supernova. I rub the familiar black fabric and follow the ice trail to the commons. I see Ivey standing there with all-white hair. And a bunch of classmates frozen in place. Alright, I've got to be confident and sure of myself. I take a deep breath and walk out of my hiding place.

"Didn't you learn the lesson the first time I beat you?" Her head snaps in my direction.

"Ah, you're back. I thought you quit the whole hero business."

"I did, but I'm back and ready to kick your ass a second time." She laughs and gets in a fighting stance. I approach her and get in a similar stance. She throws the first punch. I dodge and swing her legs out from under her. She cries out in anger and jumps back up, forming her own staff.

She swings at me, but I dodge and hit her in the knee. I hear a loud crack. She falls to one knee and screams in pain. I kick her in her good knee and watch her crumple to the floor.

Her head smacks on the ground and she's out. Her hair turns red again and I heal the bump on her head and her hurt knee. I thaw the frozen students and once they see it's me that saved them, they look happy. They rush me with a million questions. I fly up to the windows and force them open.

Clark is waiting for me when I get back home. He's looking at the news and asks, "I thought you quit. Why did you change your mind?"

"My friends were in danger and I was the only one who could stop it."

"So does this mean you're out of retirement?"

"I think so."

"Good cause this city could use the help. Now go do your homework." I nod and go to my room.

CHAPTER SIXTEEN

Felix becomes a part of our friend group over these months. He still never eats lunch. I'm still cautious about him, but he's still really polite and we've become good friends. He still walks with me to class every day. I can't stop comparing him to Olivar. We talk a lot and really connect. I feel like I might be starting to develop a crush on him. But I don't want to date anyone out of fear of them getting hurt. But if he's a vampire, he can't be killed or hurt easily.

School and life have become more bearable. Felix and I have become quite the duo. I really like him. I like spending time with him. I like listening to music with him. I like drawing him (he poses for me). I like talking to him. I just like him.

When we hang out, the hole that Olivar left when he died is almost filled again. I call Felix once I get home so we do our homework together. We always do this.

"What is the answer for number 6 on the Calculus worksheet?" he asks.

"Twenty-seven," I reply. This pattern continues throughout the evening and we joke around in between.

"Are you up for eating dinner together over video chat?" I ask.

"No, I cannot. My family is big on eating together as a big family without our phones."

"Oh okay. Well, I'm gonna go get dinner so I'll let you go." He nods and hangs up.

I go into the kitchen and heat up some leftover spaghetti and meatballs. Clark was working overtime, so I was left to fend for myself. I do kinda like the idea of family dinners but that won't happen for a long time. We need to find my sister first.

I plop down on the couch and turn on the news. They were talking about a recent spike in animal deaths around the city. Weird. I change the channel and watch *Friends*.

I hop in the shower really quickly and wash my hair. The shampoo smells like buttercream cupcakes. It's my favorite. I finish the shower and run to my room to change. I put on a hoodie and some sweatpants. I hear Clark open the door. I walk out of my room and see a man standing in the living room.

"Who the hell are you?" I ask. The person turns around and pulls out a gun. I put my hands up.

"Whoa, buddy, we're just talking. No need to whip that out."

"Give me all your money."

"No." He shoots me. I fall to the ground. Suddenly I feel a whoosh of air and the man that shot me is tackled by something or someone. I sit up and spit out the bullet. I look over at the fight happening in my living room. I see Felix on top of the man, his eyes a deep red color and his teeth sharp fangs. I was right. I join the fight.

"Oi, get him out of my house." Felix's head snaps towards me and he lets go of the man. He rushes over to me.

"Are you alright?"

"I'm fine. I can take a bullet." He looks at me, stunned. I realize my glasses came off.

"You are…you are Mirnova Tarteren."

"Yes." He bows his head.

"No, no, please don't do that. Just act like nothing happened, please." The man ran away.

Felix and I talk all night. Clark is spending the night with his girlfriend, Lucida. We were lucky it was the weekend. We talk about how his family only drinks animal blood unless they have to bite a human. That's why the news was talking about so many animal deaths.

I tell him about the times I saved the city and I finally told him what happened to Olivar. He was sympathetic. I showed him my wings and just left them out for the rest of the night. I stretch them and hear a loud pop. We laugh and continue talking. He reaches over and straightens my septum piercing. His hand lingers on my cheek. He starts to lean in. I follow his movements until our lips connect. His lips were soft and tasted faintly like metal. Blood, his lips taste like blood. But I don't really care. He pulls me so I'm straddling his hips. My wings fluff up and I wrap them around us.

He finally pulls away to catch his breath.

"That was amazing," I whisper.

"I have wanted to do that since I met you," he whispers into my hair. I kiss him again and let his hands explore my body. He reaches under my hoodie and rubs his hands up and down my back. "You're so warm," he whispered to me.

"I know." He suddenly rips my hoodie off, pulling it off my wings. I'm sitting there in just a bra as I reach over and unbutton his shirt. He helps pull it off and kisses me again. I feel him unclasp my bra. I help him take it off. He unbuttons his pants and slides them off.

He helps me slide my sweatpants off. I hope he doesn't notice my black bra doesn't match my pink panties. He pulls my panties off and slides his underwear off as well.

The whole thing is slow and soft and peaceful. It feels good, better than I can ever imagine. Feeling him inside me. We move as one and I want nothing more than to stay like this forever. I hope our neighbors don't hear us. We stay this way until the sun rises. He gets dressed and leaves through the window. I lay back on my bed and take a deep breath.

That was the best night of my life. I pull on some new clothes. I pick some pajama pants and an oversized T-shirt. I climb into bed and fall asleep

CHAPTER SEVENTEEN

I wake up around ten the next morning to Clark turning my lights on and off.

"Morning, sleepyhead. It's time to start the day." I nod and flop my head back on the pillow. I walk out into the dining room and plop down in a chair.

"You look happy."

"I was right. Felix is a vampire."

"How did you find out?" he asks.

"A man broke into our apartment and Felix came in and stopped him after the man shot me."

"How did he know something was wrong?"

"He was on a nighttime walk and heard the commotion."

"What happened after?"

"We talked through the night. He left this morning at about 5:30."

"Were you going to tell me?"

"If I said yes, would you believe me?"

"No."

"Okay, then, no." He nods and walks back into the kitchen.

I eat the breakfast Clark cooks for me and immediately run to my room. I call Ari and Lily and tell them what happened last night. We giggle and squeal for a good twenty minutes. Ari tells us that she recently had sex with her boyfriend Reed for the first time about a week ago and was trying to find a good time to tell us. We got so excited for her. Lily sighs and tells us she wishes she had a partner.

I tell her, "It's okay. The right person will find you eventually."

"Thanks, Sky."

"Anytime."

"So, do you guys want to hang out at my place?" Ari asks.

"Let me go ask Clark."

Okay, I'll go ask my mom," Lily says.

I walk into the living room and ask, "Hey, Clark, do you think I could go to Ari's for a few hours?"

"Is your homework all done?"

"Yes it is. I did it last night before that guy broke in."

"Okay, don't stay out too late and be careful."

"Will do." I salute him with two fingers and run back to my room.

"Alright, what time do you want us over?"

Ari smiles and says, "Around two will work. Does someone want to invite Felix? I'm going to invite Reed."

"I'll do it," I pipe up.

"Okay. I'll see you all around two." We hang up and I look at the time. It's only 11:30 so I have some time to kill. First I call Felix.

"Hey, Felix we're all getting together at Ari's house around two, you wanna come?"

"Sure, I would love to."

"Good, see you then." We hang up. I stand up and start to pick out an outfit, cause it'll take me a good hour or two to stop second-guessing my outfit decisions.

I finally decide on a black skater skirt, a white T-shirt, and a black cardigan. I walk into the bathroom and tame my hair. I throw it up into a messy bun. I walk out and go out and grab my glasses. My phone vibrates and I check it. I see that it's Felix.

"What do you like me better in, a polo or a button-down?"

"A button-down."

"Okay. Thanks. I'll see you soon."

"See ya." I feel butterflies rise in my stomach. This will be the first time I see him since what happened last night.

I kill time by reading a book. I read The Maze Runner. It's really good. I suddenly look at the time and see that it's 1:30. I hop up off the bed and rush out of the room. I grab my purse, slide into my white dad sneakers, and wave goodbye to Clark. The elevator was finally good for once. I got out of there in two minutes. Which never happens. I wave to Chad, who's still reading *Misery*. I really hope he likes it. It's one of my favorite Steven King novels.

I open the door and descend into the subway. The subway was busy but not too busy like it was in the morning. I hop on my train and watch as the tunnels fly by. I get off at my stop and walk the ten minutes to Ari's apartment. Her apartment is a bit fancier than mine. It has four bedrooms and a full living room and kitchen and dining room. Her parents are very famous lawyers. I've met them many times. They are super nice.

I knock on the door and it opens revealing Ari, in a navy blue cropped hoodie and some high-waisted jeans that hug her curves perfectly.

"You look nice," Ari says.

"Thanks, I love those jeans on you. They make your ass look great."

"I know, right?" She ushers me in and I see Lily and Reed already sitting on the couch. I walk inside and plop on the large, plush chair next to the couch.

After about five minutes, there's a knock at the door. Ari opens it and reveals Felix, standing there in a white button-down shirt and tan plaid pants.

"Sorry, I'm a little late, I had to finish breakfast with my family." He rubs the back of his neck. Ari pipes up.

"It's okay, silly. We were willing to wait for you." He smiles his perfect smile and sits down on the floor next to my chair.

"So what do you guys want to do?"

"We could go to the movies?" Reed says.

"I don't know. There's nothing good out right now."

"We could go to the park," Lily suggests.

"I like that idea," I say.

"Me too," Reed agrees.

"Alright, looks like we're going to the park," Ari says.

I hop up out of my chair and let Felix lead me arm in arm out the door. The walk to the park was supposed to be peaceful, but these men keep catcalling Lily. I know Lily looks older than us, with her being five foot seven, with wide hips and strong shoulders. I can see why people find her attractive, but they don't have to yell it at her. One man yells at her and Ari yells back to the man,

"SHE'S SIXTEEN!" the man looks taken aback and just lowered his head.

We finally arrive at the park and Lily runs to the swings. I join her and start swinging. She goes higher than me, but I don't care, I'm still having fun. Felix comes behind me and starts pushing me to try and get me to go higher. I giggle and kick my feet. I get a little nervous that I'm going to hit Felix.

We stop swinging and head over to the picnic tables and just hang out. I cuddle up next to Felix when I see it. A little girl running away from a grown man, tears running down her face.

"GET AWAY FROM ME! I DON'T KNOW YOU!" the kid yells and I jump into action. I run over to her and kneel down. Her chest is rising and falling rapidly and she seems terrified.

"Are you okay?"

"No, the bad man tried to take me."

"It's okay, my friends and I will protect you. Come sit with us." I grab her hand and lead her to the table.

The man approaches us and says, "Sorry, my daughter makes a fuss every time we go to leave the park. I'll take her home now."

"No, she said she doesn't know you." I hold her behind me. He goes to grab her and Felix stands in between us.

"She said no. Now you need to go before we call the cops."

"Stupid kids." He spits at us and sculks away. I turn to the little girl.

"What's your name sweetheart?"

"I'm Annabelle."

"Well, Annabelle, I'm Skylar. Do you know your mommy's phone number?"

"Yes."

"Alright, will you tell me so I can call her to come get you?" She nods and gives me the number.

"Hello, miss?"

"Hello?" the woman on the other line sounds laced with worry. "I'm here with your daughter Annabelle and we saw her run away from this man who claimed to be her father. We got her away from him and now she's safe with us at the picnic tables."

"Okay, I'm on my way." She hangs up the phone.

"Okay, sweetie, your mom's on her way." Annabelle wraps her little arms around my neck. I hug her back.

We hear footsteps and see an older woman walking up to us. Annabelle's head perks up and she goes running to the lady, saying, "Mommy, mommy, mommy!" She jumps into the woman's arms and clings to her. The woman holds her and walks up to us.

"Thank you so much for saving my little girl." She reaches into her purse and gives us each a twenty dollar bill.

"Miss, I can't take this," I say to her.

"Please, I insist. I want to show you my thanks."

"You really don't have to," I say.

"Yes, I do." I sigh and give up, pocketing the money. She smiles and walks away.

"Wow, Skylar, way to be a hero," Reed says.

I nod and say, "I couldn't stand by and watch that little girl get taken."

"That's so noble of you."

"Thanks." We all calm down after that big commotion.

After a few hours, we all decide to go home before school tomorrow. Clark greets me when I walk through the door.

"Welcome back. How was hanging out with your squad?"

"Please never say the word *squad* ever again. But I had a good time."

"Alright, good. Now get ready for bed. You have school in the morning."

"I know, I know." I walk into my room and grab my towels. I walk into the bathroom and turn on the hot water. The water steams and I step under it. It feels so good. I take a deep breath and let the shower calm me before bed. My God I talk about my showers a lot. And always talk about how I fall asleep. Man, I'm predictable.

Once I'm done, I hop out and rush into my room. I put on my oversized sweatshirt and sweatpants. The second my head hits the pillow, I'm out.

CHAPTER EIGHTEEN

I wake up and look outside. It's raining. Yes! I love the rain. I hear Clark groan from the hallway.

"Dammit. It's raining."

"What do you mean 'dammit'? Rain is the best."

Just wait till you have to walk twenty blocks to get to your job in it."

"Okay, that makes sense."

"Yeah, now get ready. You don't want to be late." I nod and close the door so I can change.

I change into a black T-shirt dress, black tights, and a gray cardigan. Clark is making bacon. I can smell it. It smells so good. I walk out to the small table and sit down, waiting for the glorious bacon to be done. Clark finally finishes and places my plate in front of me. I giggle and dig in. It tastes amazing.

I finish eating, pull on my shoes and backpack and leave. The elevator was the worst it has ever been. It takes us a solid fifteen minutes to get to the first floor. (My God I also talk about my elevator a lot). I wave to Chad, and bolt to the subway. I rush to my train and wait for it to move. I people watch while on the train. A few seats down I see Ivey, crying. It takes everything in me not to be mean to her. I walk over and sit next to her.

"Hey, Ivey. Are you okay?"

"Go away, freak."

"No. You're upset and I want you to know that if you want to, you can talk to me."

"Really? Even after I've been so mean to you?"

"Yes."

"Well, my parents are getting divorced and I want to live with my dad, but my mom is really mad and she called me a stupid, selfish bitch just before I left for school today." I grab her hand.

"I am so sorry that is happening to you. You don't deserve this." I rub her back and let her cry.

"Do you want to walk to school with me? Maybe I can take you to the counselor."

"I'd like that.

Our stop comes, and I wrap an arm around Ivey's shoulders and walk her into school. Our friends stare at us but I don't care. I help her to the counselor. The counselor lets me go to my class and takes Ivey to her office.

I walk out and immediately collide with my friends.

"What was that?" Ari asks me.

"I found Ivey on the subway, sobbing her eyes out and I just had to help her."

"But she's a bitch."

"And I'm not." Lily sighs and the bell rings. We all disperse to our different classes. Felix runs up to me.

"I think the way you helped Ivey was truly splendid. Not everyone would be able to do that to someone who harmed them before."

"Thanks." I smile at him and he opens the door for me again.

I don't see Ivey for the rest of the day. I know she's been really mean to me in the past, but I just feel like I should help her. My friends have gotten over it cause Lily says, "That's just the way Sky is." Everyone agrees and finally lets it go. We eat lunch in peace until Jessica comes stomping over.

"What the hell were you doing with MY bff this morning?"

"She was sobbing on the same train as me and I couldn't just sit there and watch her be upset so I helped her."

"Are you trying to steal my bestie?"

"No, just trying to help someone in need."

"Good." She stomps away and I let out a breath.

Lunch finishes and we head to the next class. Once school is over I walk home and flop on my bed. I groan loudly and hear Clark chuckle from the living room.

"You okay in there?"

"*Uggghhh!*"

"Okay."

I sit up and start my homework. Felix FaceTimes me for our usual homework study sesh.

"Hey, Skylar, do you think I could ask you a question?"

"Yeah, go ahead."

"Do you want to be my girlfriend?" My pencil drops. Of course I say yes. He smiles and runs his fingers through his hair.

I smile at him and say, "You're the first guy I've liked since my other boyfriend was killed, so please be wary of some things. Because some things you do might remind me of him and I'll get sad, but I'll try to push past that sadness and focus on the happiness of our new relationship, but it might take me a bit to get used to it."

"I completely understand. You do not get over something like that. I will make sure that I am accommodating." I smile wider and nearly scream.

"Do you want to go out on a date this weekend?" he asks.

"Yes. I would love that." He smiles and hangs up. I flop back on the bed and squeal.

I immediately call Ari and Lily and we freak out for a solid five minutes. Ari congratulates me and Lily says, "Finally, the romantic tension between you two was thick with three Cs." I giggle at her words.

"Alright I gotta get back to homework," Ari says. We all agree and hang up. A few minutes later, Clark comes and knocks on the door.

"Come in." He opens the door. "So, do I get to know what all the squealing and giggling was about?"

"I have a boyfriend and we're going on a date this weekend. As long as that's okay with you."

"Is it with the vampire?"

"Maybe."

He sighs and thinks for a few seconds. "Just be super careful. I don't want to see you on the news, your body sucked dry of all its blood."

"He and his family are different. They only eat animal blood."

"Good. Well go finish your homework. I'll have dinner ready soon."

"Okay." I walk back to my room and finish my homework. Clark makes mac and cheese for dinner and it tastes amazing. I devour two plates.

CHAPTER NINETEEN

The week went by at a snail's pace, but Saturday came at last. I wake up with so much excitement. I hop out of bed and run to the bathroom. I turn on a hype playlist and jam out while brushing my teeth. Clark walks by, rolls his eyes, and chuckles. I ignore him and continue getting ready.

Felix told me to dress for a picnic so I choose a plain white crop top, light wash mom jeans, and a long, black cardigan. I braid my hair into two french braids and walk into the living room.

"Well, how do I look?" I ask Clark. He peels his eyes away from the TV and looks me up and down.

"Looks good."

"Thanks." I pull on my creepers and grab my bag.

The elevator was, for the first time ever, empty. I sigh and lean back against the back of the elevator. It stops at the first floor and I step out to see Felix standing there with a basket and a hot pink blanket.

"Hey, there you are. Are you ready?" I nod as he takes my hand and leads me out the building. His pale skin softly glitters in the sunlight. We walk arm in arm to the park and find a nice place to sit down.

He lays the blanket out and sets the basket down.

"You gave my mother an excuse to use the kitchen for the first time." He pulls out a sandwich and a bottle of "cranberry juice." He passes me the sandwich and takes a sip of his "cranberry juice." I bite down on the sandwich and instantly regret doing that. I spit it out and wipe my tongue with my sleeve.

"No offense but your mom is not good at making food."

"Eh, it was her first time. I'm sorry."

"It's okay I'll go get a hot dog from that cart over there."

"Let me pay for it," he insists.

"Um…okay." He walks with me and he buys me a hot dog.

We sit back down and just talk. We talk about anything and everything. We talk about school. We talk about music. We talk about books. I could listen to his voice forever. The date goes better after we both finish our "breakfast." We head to a Broadway show. He got tickets for my favorite show, *Phantom of the Opera*. We sit down and watch the marvelous show. I love every minute of it. Felix keeps looking at me and smiling. He took me to a wonderful restaurant called The Silver Dragon. It's a Japanese steak house.

We sit down and I order food. The steak here is delicious. I would recommend this place to so many people. Felix doesn't eat, as usual, but he seems content watching me enjoy my food. He pays and walks me back home. He kisses me before leaving to go home. I smile and walk up to our apartment.

Clark notices the blush in my cheeks when I open the door.

"Did something I won't like happen?"

"No, we just kissed."

"Okay." I walk into my room and flop on my bed. I smile to myself. That was one of the best days of my life. He really knows how to make me happy and I hope I know how to make him happy too. He seemed happy, so I'm not really worried. I think this whole thing is going to work out.

CHAPTER TWENTY

Winter has come, (Love *Game of Thrones*), and it is freezing. Not for me, though. It pays off to have your body full of fire. I walk to lunch with a giant jacket in my arms.

We all sit down and start eating; then Ivey walks up to us.

"Do any of you know of a way to contact Supernova?" They all look at me. I got an idea.

"Actually yes. I heard she's started a phone line for people who need help. I'll give you the number." She visibly relaxed.

"Thank you so much, Skylar." I hand her my phone number and watch her leave. Luckily, I have a voice changing spell so she won't recognize my voice over the phone.

I head home and after about ten minutes, I get a phone call from a number I don't recognize. I instantly cast the voice changing spell and answer the call.

"Hello?"

"Hello, this is the new Supernova hotline. What is your emergency?"

"It's a long story, could you send her to Thomas Jefferson High School, so I may explain?"

"Hold on, let me talk to her."

"Okay." I press Hold and think this through. On one hand she could just be calling me there to attack me or she could really need help. The way she was during lunch when she asked for the phone number suggests the latter. I decide to go and see what she wants.

I transform and fly to the school. She was there, sitting on the frozen fountain looking nervous. I land in front of her and she jumps. She doesn't seem to be cold. I guess that makes sense.

"You wanted to speak with me."

"Ye…yes I need help. My family is cursed and I need help breaking it."

"What kind of curse?"

"Many, many generations ago a woman of my family line rudely rejected a man whose sister was a witch. The sister cursed the woman that all the females of her bloodline would be cursed with a frozen heart. Basically we're cursed with ice powers and we are cursed to be rude and bitchy to everyone. I've bullied people my whole life because I don't know how to be nice because of this curse. Will you help me find the descendant of this witch and get the curse broken."

"I would love to help you. I want to show you something. You have to keep my secret, because if you don't, many people I love will get hurt and I will hunt you down to the ends of the earth. Do you understand?' She nods and I detransform.

Ivey looks at me in shock.

"You're Supernova?!? I was not expecting that. Well, you're still an ugly bitch. Sorry, I really didn't want to say that."

"Well, now I know you couldn't help it. You were literally cursed." She smiles sadly and tucks a piece of hair behind her ear.

"Now, where are we working?"

"You can come to my apartment. My parents don't mind when I randomly bring friends over." I nod and follow her.

CHAPTER TWENTY-ONE

We walk to the subway and head over to Ivey's house. Her apartment is nice, not as nice as Ari's, but very nice. She leads me to her room. She has a beautiful landscape accent wall.

"Did you paint that?"

"Yes."

"You are really good. Are you in any art classes at school, because you should be."

"Thanks and I am. I love to draw and paint."

"Me too."

"Really?"

"Yeah."

We sit down on her lush, white bed.

"Alright, what do we know about this witch?"

"Her family name is Rottin. Their family is from Upstate New York. The last witch in their family is named Alanna. I just need to find her and ask her to reverse the curse." She sighs. I get out my phone and google "Alanna Rottin NYC," then wait for anything to come up. A link to an Instagram profile of a woman whose bio reads, "Witchy vibes only. Don't be rude to me or something might happen to you."

"This looks like we got our person. She posted a picture of her at her school. She goes to—"

"Hurry up, freak! Sorry, force of habit."

"It's alright. You are cursed after all."

"Why are you being so nice to me? I've done nothing but bully you."

I turn to her. "I believe there is good in everyone. No matter what they've done to me, everyone deserves a second chance."

"Thank you, freak."

"You're welcome, bitch." We smile. "Now the school she goes to is Tuck Hall Academy. "Alright, on Monday, call out from school and I'll do the same and we'll go talk to her at her school."

"I like that plan. Do you maybe want to stay here tonight?"

"Sure. You know what, Ivey, I think, once we break this curse, you and I are going to be good friends."

"I'd like that. Now, do you want to do a face mask and watch a movie?"

"I'd love to, just let me tell my brother."

I quickly text Clark and he says to just be careful and have fun. Ivey comes back in with a basket of sheet masks.

"Okay, go ahead and pick any one you want. She turns on the TV mounted on the wall and goes to Netflix.

"So, what should we watch?" she asks.

"How about *Midnight Sun*."

"Okay!" She turns it on and we help each other put on our sheet masks. Mine smells like coconuts and pineapple. Ivey's smelled like strawberries.

We watch the movie and cry at the ending. If you've seen the movie, you know. She lends me some pj's and only calls me freak three more times and she apologizes every time, so it looks like she's trying to fight against her curse. We go to bed and prepare for the conversation we are going to have with this Alanna.

CHAPTER TWENTY-TWO

We walk up the steps of the academy and spot her. She had honey blonde hair, high cheekbones and ocean blue eyes. We walk up to her and pull her away from her friends.

"Who the hell are you people?"

"Your ancestor cursed mine and I need you to reverse it."

"Ah, you're a Van Pel. Why should I? Your ancestor deserved it."

"But I'm not my ancestor."

"Alright. I'll break the curse if you go on a date with my brother."

"I'll do it." Alanna pulls out her cell phone and calls her brother, Alex, to come where we are. A boy with the same hair, cheekbones, and eyes as Alanna walks over to us. He was pretty handsome and fit.

"Alex, this is Ivey Van Pel and you are going on a date with her so then I will break the curse on her family."

"Alright. Hey, I'm Alex." Ivey looks at him and smiles.

"So, are you free this Saturday?"

"Yeah. You wanna meet at Uno Mas around four?"

"Yeah, that works for me."

As we walk away, I clap Ivey on the shoulder.

"Wow, you didn't even need me. You did that all by yourself. I'm so happy for you."

"Thanks. Do you think once this curse is broken, I could hang out with you and your friends. I don't think I want to be friends with people like Jessica."

"It might take my friends a bit to accept you, but we can try."

She smiles. "Jessica's gonna be pissed at me."

"Yeah, don't worry about her. I'll handle her. She can be a bitch. Hey,

I'm sorry for pouring water on you that one time. It was Jess's idea, but I just went along with it. I'm sorry."

"Wow, are you sure the curse isn't already broken?"

"I don't know. I don't feel any different. I still want to call you a freak every time I address you."

"Alright, maybe not." We burst out into laughter.

"Well, I should probably get home. I'll see you later." She waves as I walk away.

I close the apartment door and run to my room. I hear Clark open the door.

"I better have a good reason for calling you out today."

"I was helping someone break a curse on their family."

"Oh, okay. Well, be sure to do your makeup work."

"Will do." I collapse onto my bed and breathe in the fresh scent of our laundry detergent.

Ari comes by and gives me my missed work. I work on it for the rest of the night.

CHAPTER TWENTY-THREE

I finish my makeup work in a few hours. It was pretty easy to understand. Clark calls me into the small dining room for dinner. He made chicken and rice. I eat it happily.

"So was your day off productive?"

"Yeah. I'm helping someone break a curse on her family. She's going on a date and then the last witch in the family that cursed the other girl's family is going to reverse the curse."

"That's good. Tell her I hope the curse gets reversed."

"Will do." We continue eating in silence.

I take a shower and quickly change into some soft pajama pants and one of Clark's old T-shirts. Lily calls me about ten minutes after I get out of the shower.

"Hey, girl, we missed you in school today. I heard you're helping Ivey break some curse on her family."

"Yeah and once the curse is broken she wants to be our friend."

"I don't know."

"She's actually not that bad once you crack away at her outer shell."

"I'll give her a chance, after the curse is broken."

"Good. Well, I'll see you tomorrow."

"See ya." I hang up and breathe. I'm glad my friends are willing to give Ivey a chance. I climb under the covers and go to sleep.

I wake up with a little more pep in my step. I get dressed in some baggy mom jeans and a large, baggy, long-sleeved shirt. I throw my hair up in a low ponytail and grab my glasses.

Clark calls me out for breakfast. I walk out and take a seat. He sits down after handing me a plate of bacon and eggs.

"So, Lucinda and I are going on a business trip for a few days. Will you be able to handle things by yourself for a bit?"

"Yeah, I'll be fine.'

"Okay good. If you need me at any time just call."

"Will do." We continue our breakfast.

I place my plate in the sink and run out the door, after putting on my shoes and grabbing my bag. I wave bye to Chad and run to the subway. Standing there was Ivey. Her face lit up when she saw me. She ran over to me.

"Hey, do you want to ride the train together?"

"Sure. You are doing a really good job at being nice even with the curse."

"I'm trying."

"Well, you're doing a good job."

"Thanks." We board the train and sit together. We talk about a bunch of different things. I found out she likes K-pop like me. Her favorite band is Exo. We gush over how hot the K-pop stars are and make a promise to try and go to the next concert together.

We arrive at school and go our separate ways. Ari looks a little suspicious.

"I can't believe you actually are being nice to her. She's been mean to us since first grade."

"She's cursed to be mean to everyone. She can't help it. I'm trying to help her become a better person. Just give her a chance."

Ari crosses her arms and thinks. "Fine, but the second she starts acting like a bitch, she's out."

I smile. "Alright, she's going to slowly separate herself from her current friends and come over to our group and will be fully over on our side by the time the curse is broken." They all nod and the bell rings. We all head off to our different classes.

CHAPTER TWENTY-FOUR

Ivey comes over to my apartment to get ready for her date. She brought her giant makeup kit. I lead her to my bathroom and watch her do her makeup flawlessly.

"Wow, you're really good. Remind me to call you to do my makeup when I go out with Felix."

"Thanks and I would love to do your makeup sometime." We turn on a K-pop playlist and jam out.

Once she's done I start brushing her hair.

"Alright, what do you want me to do with your hair?"

"The dress I'm wearing has pretty flowers and is very flowy, so maybe a braid crown with little pieces framing my face. And we should curl those pieces."

"Okay." I start braiding her pretty copper hair.

"I love your hair color."

"Thanks."

Once I'm done braiding, I facepalm.

"I don't have a curling iron."

"But you do have a high body temperature and your fingers."

"That's a good idea." I move some of the heat in my body to my fingers and curl her hair around them. The hair falls into pretty ringlets.

"Perfect. Now, let's see your dress." I walk out of the bathroom to let her change in private.

She walks out in a white dress with purple and blue flowers and green leaves. It looked beautiful on her.

"You look amazing."

"Thanks." I look at the time.

"It's 3:50. You gotta go. You don't want to be late."

"Right." She nods and grabs her purse and slides into her flats.

"Alright, come back here once it's over. I want all the details."

"Of course." She rushes out the door and heads out to Uno Mas.

I lounge around the house for the next few hours, reading a good book. I also turned on *Kitchen Nightmares*. I love watching Gordon Ramsay yell at incompetent people.

After three hours I hear a knock at the door. I open it to see Ivey with a happy, wistful smile on her face.

"Did you have a good time?" I ask.

"Yes, we got along well enough, but he's not really my type. We decided to just be friends."

I smile at her. "That's great. Now do you want to get in our pj's, do some face masks, and watch *Twilight*?"

"You read my mind." I change in my room, and Ivey changes in the bathroom. I change into one of Felix's hoodies and some sweatpants. Ivey walks into the living room in a silk pajama set that was a pale pink color.

We sit down on the couch and turn on *Twilight*. Ivey pulls out her gargantuan box of sheet masks. I pick the honey sheet mask. Ivey has to help me put it on correctly. We curl up on the couch with some blankets and watch *Twilight*.

CHAPTER TWENTY-FIVE

Ivey's curse was finally broken and she has become an integral part of our friend group. Jessica is pissed at us for "stealing" her friend. Ivey tells her many times that she doesn't want to be her friend anymore. The others are slow to accept her into our group at first, but over time they grow to like her.

We are sitting at lunch, chatting. Ari throws a fry at me to get me out of my thoughts. I perk my head up and turn to her.

"What's up?"

"Ivey wanted to know if you wanted to have a sleepover with us at her place this weekend."

"Yeah. I'd love to." I smile.

"Awesome. I just got some new sheet masks from South Korea. They're really good for your skin."

The boys look so uninterested in our skincare endeavors. They make their own plans that don't involve us. My mind wanders back to Ivey. I'm just so happy her curse is broken. Jessica's thoughts make their way into my head. *I can't believe Ivey left me for those freaks.* My smile drops a bit, but I tune back in to the conversation.

Lunch goes by and we all walk to class. I head to drawing class. Mrs. Clay is wearing a flowing skirt and a long T-shirt. She is also wearing Jesus sandals. I still love Mrs. Clay and her wacky personality. She's super supportive and accepting about anything and everything.

I work on my drawing of cherry blossom trees on a long path. Mrs. Clay walks around the class nodding and hyping students up. She gets to me and says that the cherry blossom trees look just like the ones she saw in Japan. I smile and continue working.

School finally ends and I'm walking home when I hear this big explosion.

I look up and see a fire blazing in the building above me. I hear people screaming for help. I run to the alley and transform.

The people screaming and waving out the window look relieved when I fly into their line of sight. I start grabbing people and flying them down to the ground. Suddenly there was another explosion. I peel back the broken metal window frames and push myself into the building.

The fire is raging and spreading fast. I look around for more people and find a few women huddled in a corner. I help them out of the building and go back in.

The stairwell was falling apart more and more by the second. A piece of railing falls and nearly takes off my head. Luckily, I move in time. People's screams echo above me and I try to fly up the small stairwell. My wings get caught on the railings what feels like a thousand times.

I reach the upper floors and start breaking windows to help people get out. It takes a good twenty minutes and a lot of close calls, but I eventually get everyone out of the building.

I try to pull all the fire towards me and out of the building. Thankfully, it works and I can disperse the fire up into the sky. The fire bursts into a firework. I climb back inside and look around the melted frame of this office building.

Sitting in the middle of the room is a busted up shell of a bomb. And a few feet to the left was another bomb.

"What the hell?" I whisper. "Who the hell would bomb a random office building?" The smell of gunpowder hangs in the air like a thick fog. I cough and gag and nearly vomit.

Suddenly the door swings open. "Supernova, what are you doing here?" I cough more and raise my pointer finger.

"I helped everyone get out of the building. There's bombs here. Warning: the gunpowder is thick in the air." I go into another coughing fit. The cops cough as well, trying to hold cloths over their faces.

"Did everyone get out?" one of the cops yells. I nod. They all come in and look around at the charred smokey, foggy shell of an office building.

"Do you know who set the bombs off?" the officer asks. I shake my head. "Well, I'm glad you got everyone out. You may leave now." I nod in thanks and climb out the melted window.

The flight home was short, thankfully. I changed into some pajamas the minute I got home. Clark has a late-night at work, so I am left by myself for dinner. I heat up some leftover pasta and sit down on the couch. I turned on the news, knowing they would be talking about the bombing.

The pretty reporter with long, perfectly wavy, caramel hair is standing next to a dark-skinned man in a white shirt covered in soot. He was describing the bombing in detail.

"And then out of nowhere, like a guardian angel, she appeared. Supernova. She saved my life and the lives of so many others. I would be dead if not for her. Supernova, if you're out there watching, thank you. From all you saved today, thank you."

I smiled and the reporter went to talk to another person. That person thanked me as well. It felt so good to help people. I feel like a real hero. I hope I can keep helping people like this forever.

I stay up a bit later than normal cause it is a Friday night. I put on *Kitchen Nightmares* and scroll through TikTok; then Clark walks in the door. He rubs his eyes and hangs his coat on the hanger.

"Rough day?" I ask. I didn't like the look on his face.

"Yeah. My boss is a dick and assigned me four articles to write by Monday." I stand up and go and rub his shoulder.

"I'm sorry. Do you want me to heat you up something to eat?" I smile kindly. He shakes his head.

"Okay. Did you see the news?"

"Yes, I am so proud of you. Your first big rescue. How do you feel?"

I smile and blush. "I feel great."

He nods and walks off to take a shower.

CHAPTER TWENTY-SIX

There have been three more bombing in random office buildings all around the city. I try to save everyone from the flames, but some people still die. I feel awful when I can't save someone.

The government is involved now as these are now seen as terrorist attacks. I agree but of course people are being shitty and blaming certain groups of people when we don't even know who is bombing these buildings.

I'm walking to the subway when I see the strange bald boy for the first time. He had a swastika with a red background on his jacket. I instantly dislike him. I stay as far away from him as possible.

I meet up with Ivey and we ride the train together. That's where I see the boy again. He seems to pull something out of his pocket. He hurries off at the next stop. I look at the thing he put on the floor and a chill runs down my spine. I run over to it and clutch it to my chest.

Ivey yells after me and runs out of the train as I run up the stairs onto the streets. I rush into an alleyway and summon my wings. I fly up and let the bomb in my arms explode. The fire engulfs me and absorbs into my skin. I see fiery cracks appear on my arms and legs. I fall to the ground and land in that alley.

I hide my wings and walk back out onto the streets. Ivey finds me and asks, and I quote,
"What the flippity-floppity-fuck was that?"

I place my hand on her shoulder. "That bald kid put a bomb in the subway and I had to get it out of the subway and away from the city. I think it's the new generation of Nazis behind the bombing. I saw the boy before I got on the train and he had a swastika on his jacket."

"We should tell the cops. Or Supernova should tell the cops." I nod and grab her arm, dragging her back down to the subway. We can't be late.

We weren't late, thank God, and school flies by. We make it to lunch and sit at our usual table.

"We know who's behind the bombings," Ivey says as we sit down. Lily, Ari, Reed, and Felix look at us, shocked. We chatter away and make sure to whisper so no one else can hear us.

I rush to the cops after school. I run as fast as I can in my platform boots. I guess I forgot I can fly. The cops listen to what I have to say and tell me they're gonna look into this Nazi hate group that's been growing in numbers lately. I nod happily and walk out the door.

I fly home and eat dinner.

CHAPTER TWENTY-SEVEN

My room is frigid when I wake up the next day.

"CLARK, DID THE HEAT BREAK?" I yell.

He pops his head in my doorframe.

"No, do you want me to turn it up?"

"Yes please." He nods and walks back to the living room. The hot air blasts out of the vents leaving a faint musty smell in my room. I tuck the comforter up under my chin and try to warm up, moving the fire within me out into my whole body.

Luckily, I warm up quickly and I climb out of bed and walk out for breakfast. When I walk out, I see Clark sitting at the desk in the living room furiously typing on his computer. Guess I'm on my own for breakfast. I raid the pantry and end up making instant ramen, the breakfast of champions.

I sit in my room with my ramen and Netflix on my laptop. Suddenly the building shakes. I stand up and run into the living room. That's when I start to smell the thick, heavy, weight of smoke coming from outside the door. Someone must've followed me home when I flew back. I grab Clark and wrap his arms around my neck.

Summoning my wings, I fly out a window on the backside of the building. We land on the ground and I change into my superhero clothes. Before I go up to help the rest of the people in the building, Clark grabs my arm.

"Please be careful." He looks worried.

"Always am." He smiles and lets me go. I fly up and start helping people out of the building. This whole thing is chaos. The fire department gets here quickly and I help them put out the fire.

Clark and I were lucky and the fire didn't touch our apartment, so we can still get our stuff to move somewhere safer. Clark luckily knows a landlord who has an apartment open with two bedrooms and one bathroom and it's ours if we want it. He says he saw the story of the explosion on TV and wants to help in any way he can.

We go to our new apartment that is just a few minutes' walk from our old apartment. I spend the rest of my day decorating my new room. It is actually a little bigger than my old room. I hang up my posters and Christmas lights and my tapestries. It looks very cute if I do say so myself.

Clark pops his head in and asks what I want for dinner. I say we should just order pizza. He agrees and calls in the order. My new room looks fucking awesome. I love it so much.

Clark calls me out for dinner and we sit on the couch watching the news, eating our pizza. The pretty news reporter is back talking about the bombing of our old building.

About three minutes later, I get calls from my friends. They all are so worried and just want to check up on me and make sure I'm okay. I tell them we're at a friend of Clark's building. They all noticeably relax over the phone. I tell them to stop worrying and go to bed before school in the morning.

After I finish my dinner, I walk into our new bathroom and take a shower. It is nice and warm. I wash my hair and sing along to my playlist and dance badly.

Once I'm done with my shower I walk to my room and change into some boxer shorts and a T-shirt. I climb into bed in my new room that glows a soft golden light. It starts to rain and the sound of rain against my window slowly rocks me to sleep.

I wake up and freak out for a second, thinking I've been kidnapped or something, but then I remember the events of yesterday. I groan, remembering it's Monday. I climb out of bed and go brush my teeth and hair. Ugggh! I hate Mondays. I just want to go back to sleep.

I finish up in the bathroom and head to my new closet. It's a walk-in closet. I pull on some black, ripped, mom jeans and a white and gray baseball tee.

Clark hasn't moved since last night. He fell asleep on his keyboard. I go up and tap him on the shoulder. His head pops up and he looks confused.

"Morning, sleepyhead."

"Morning." I walk into the kitchen and pull out some cereal and a bowl. I grab the milk out of the fridge as well and I pour the cereal first because I'm not insane. Clark turned on the morning news for us to watch.

I settle on the couch with my breakfast and watch the reporters covering the story of the bombings. Things are really getting out of hand. I've decided I'm going to find that bald boy and make him and his group stop. I might see him on the way to school today. I finish my breakfast and put my bowl in the sink. Clark gets up from his chair and goes to the bathroom for the first time since midnight. I walk over to the shoe rack and pull on my black Converse. I grab my bag and head out the door.

The elevator ride here is much better. I could get used to this. I greet our new doorman.

"Sir, what's your name?" He looks taken aback. I guess no one really asks him that.

"Well, my name is Steve." He smiles and offers his hand. I take it and shake.

"I'm Skylar, but most people call me Sky." I smile at him as well and start to walk away. I open the door and get blasted with cold December air. I spread my fire around my body and run to the subway. Luckily I still have to take the same train to get to school.

I meet up with Ivey and she floods me with what feels like a thousand questions. I eventually get her to calm down and explain everything that happened yesterday.

She listens carefully, nodding along and visibly relaxing when I say we found a place to live.

"If you didn't find a place, I was gonna offer my place until you find a more permanent address." I smile and thank her. We chat some more and get off at our stop.

Everyone at school looks at me with sympathy and worried looks. I try so hard to ignore them, but it's really difficult. I just wish they would mind their own business.

I walk to my first class and Felix tries to distract me from all the people staring at me. He takes my hands and rubs the fleshy part between my thumb and pointer finger. I smile at him and he kisses my forehead.

The teacher starts talking and thankfully everyone stops staring at me. I listen intently to the teacher and try to not let my mind wander.

CHAPTER TWENTY-EIGHT

Ivey and I are walking to the train home when I see him again. The bald boy. I want to transform and tackle him. He's not wearing his Nazi jacket this time, but I will never forget his face.

I quickly pull out my phone and call the nonemergency line and tell them I saw one of the potential bombers. They say they're sending someone right away.

Now, I need to keep him here until the cops get here. I walk up to him and say, "Hey, I've seen you around with a certain jacket. Can you explain to me the meaning of the jacket?" he smiles at me and starts spewing out hate speech towards Jewish people and LGBTQ+ people.

After about five minutes talking with this guy, I hear the sirens. The cops make it and jump out of the car. I grab the boy's arm to make sure he doesn't run.

I drag him over to the cops, him fighting me the whole way there.

"Here he is." I hand him over to the cops, and he starts yelling hate speech at me.

"I'll bomb all of you just like I did to the others." That was enough for the cops to make an arrest.

They take him away and I sigh in relief. Hopefully that's the end of the bombings. I didn't even need to be Supernova to catch him. I told the cops I don't want my name involved in any of this. They nod and say that's okay.

Ivey and I walk to the train and she is celebrating with me that the bombings can finally stop.

Clark is standing in the living room when I get home.

"Did you hear they caught the bomber?"

"Yeah, I called the cops on him, but I asked them to not use my name or involve me in any of this." He nods and hugs me.

"I'm so proud of the person you've become. Mom and Dad would be too." I smile and hug him back.

"Okay, I'm gonna go make dinner." I nod and walk into my room and start my homework.

Clark makes chicken for dinner and we sit in our new, slightly bigger, dining room and eat together. The chicken is delicious and I enjoy it thoroughly.

CHAPTER TWENTY-NINE

Felix runs after me as I exit the school on this cold and rainy Thursday afternoon. I turn to him as he yells my name

"Hey, Sky, my family is having a fancy gala and told me to invite my girlfriend cause they want to meet you. It's this Saturday. Will you come?"

"What should I wear?" He smiles and says a formal gown will be best. I might have to ask my mom if she has anything. I don't really have any formal gowns. I get home and summon my mom. She was wearing a flowy rose gold gown with jewels on the front and long sleeves.

"Hello, Moondrop. Is everything alright?"

"Yes, it's just I need a gown for a vampire gala with my boyfriend, but I don't have anything even close to formal enough. Do you maybe have anything?"

"Yes, I think I do. Take my hand." I do so and suddenly I'm standing in the most grand bedroom I have ever seen. She pulls me into the closet and pulls out a long black dress with short, wrap-like sleeves, a lace-up back, and a flowy tulle skirt.

"It's perfect. Thanks, Mom." She pulls me into a hug.

"Now to get it to fit you there is a spell in the book I gave you that will make it fit perfectly to your body. I hope you have fun with your boyfriend. When do I get to meet him?"

"Soon. I'm meeting his parents for the first time at this gala. I'm really nervous that they won't like me."

"If they have any sort of brain, they'll love you." She kisses me on the head and magics me back into my room. I put the dress on a hanger in my closet and start my homework.

My mind wanders to how I am going to do my hair and makeup for the gala. I call Ivey, knowing she has a giant makeup kit.

"Hey, Ivey, I'm going to a gala with Felix this Saturday night and need someone to do my makeup. Can you help me?"

"I would love to." I smile and thank her. I hang up and try to get back to my homework. I finish and go out to eat dinner. I have ramen again cause Clark's working late again. I go back to thinking about how I want to do my hair for Felix's parent's gala. I think I'll do a fancy fishtail braid.

The rest of the week flies by and before I know it, it's Saturday. I hear a knock on our door around 4:00 p.m. The gala starts at seven.

I open the door and see Ivey standing there with her makeup bags in her hands. I let her in and we head to the bathroom. Ivey looks at the dress and comes up with a makeup look that will compliment both the dress and my features.

She gets started and we chat about our favorite TV shows. I gush about how much I love *Merlin*. Ivey says she's never seen it so I make a mental note to make her watch it with me sometime. Ivey talks about *RuPaul's Drag Race*. I also love that show. Those people are so talented and amazingly dedicated to what they do. We finish my makeup and I start to do my hair. I braid my hair back and pull out some pieces to frame my face and fluff my bangs.

Ivey helps me lace up the dress. It is a little big so I pull out my special book and find the spell my mom was talking about. The dress suddenly forms perfectly to my body. I pull on my black mary janes and look at the time. It's six fifteen.

Felix said he was sending a car to pick me up. I head downstairs and wait for the car. Steve says I look pretty and I say thank you. I hear a car pull up and I walk to the window. The window rolls down and a very pale man sits in the driver's seat.

"Skylar Kent?" I nod and he tells me to hop in. We drive off. The inside of the car was luxurious. Red seats, black dashboard, fresh new car smell, and velvet seat covers. I rub the velvet nervously as we drive to Felix's house.

We pull up to this modern mansion. It is beautiful. I see through the windows a shit ton of people in fancy dresses and suits. Once we make it to the front door the driver walks over to my side of the car and opens the door for me. I step out and see Felix standing by the doorway.

He sees me and walks over to me. He smiles and offers me his arm. I smile back and take it.

"My parents want to meet you right away. Don't worry, they'll love you."

He squeezes my arm and we walk inside. Inside there were grand chandeliers and long tables of food and blood bags. There were so many people of varying magical races.

Felix leads me to the center of the main hall where two older vampires stand. The woman is slender but still has beautiful curves. She is wearing a wine red dress with a slit on the side. Her hair is dark and spilling over her shoulders in gorgeous waves. Next to her is a tall vampire man with dark hair smoothed back on his head. He is wearing a pressed black suit and a large smile. His smile is just like Felix's.

We walk up to the couple and Felix does a little flourish with his hand. "Mom, Dad, this is my girlfriend, Skylar." His mom looks me up and down and smiles.

"Hello. I'm Victoria." She cups my cheeks and kisses them both. "You are just as cute as a button. I love your dress. It's beautiful."

"Thanks, I got it from my mom."

His father looks at me and asks, "What kind of creature are you?"

"Umm, I'm actually Princess Mirnova." Their jaws drop. "You can't tell anyone. My uncle is still looking for me and if he knew I was dating your son, he could get hurt."

They nod and smile. "We won't tell a soul." His dad takes my hand and asks, "Will you dance with me, Skylar?" I blush.

"Sure, Mr. Gifford."

"Please call me William." He pulls me towards the large ballroom-like space where there were many people dancing. William grabs my hand and leads me into the dance floor. He smiles at me.

"So, my son seems completely entranced by you. Did you cast a spell on him or something? I've never seen him this happy with someone."

"No, no spells. And I adore your son. I was in a really dark place when I met your son. My previous boyfriend was killed in front of me and I became severely depressed. Felix really is my light at the end of the tunnel." He smiles at me and spins me back over to Felix and his wife. Felix takes my arm from his father and tells me he wants to introduce me to some of his friends.

He introduces me to this pretty, tall werewolf girl with long caramel hair, sharp gray eyes, and legs that went on forever. She was super nice and had the personality of a golden retriever. Her name was Mira.

Felix leads me to a group of demon boys who were throwing food at each other. "Guys, guys, calm down. I want you all to meet someone." They all look at me. "This is Skylar Kent. My girlfriend. Skylar, this is Raymond, Goldof, Baelfire, and Tramon." Raymond was tall, not as tall as Felix. He had wine-colored eyes and dark brown hair. Goldof was short compared to his friends. With pale amber eyes and white blond hair. Baelfire was average height with inky black hair and an olive complexion. Tramon was the tallest, even taller than Felix. With stoic brown eyes and buzz-cut dirty blond hair.

"These boys are my best friends in the supernatural world. I've known them since I was three."

"It's nice to meet you guys. I'm Skylar, but most people call me Sky."

"Hi, Sky. I'm Raymond. It's so nice to finally meet you. Felix hasn't stopped talking about you since he met you. I love your dress. Don't you think so, honey?" He turns to Baelfire.

"Yes, it looks beautiful on you, miss."

"Thank you. Am I allowed to ask if you two are together?"

"Yes, we are. Baelfire is my boyfriend and I could not ask for a better partner."

I smile and Felix starts to take me to see other people. By the end of the night, I'm all peopled out. I just want to go home and go to sleep, but it would be rude to leave in the middle of the gala. I escaped for a few minutes in the bathroom. I take a moment to calm down and collect myself. Luckily my makeup and hair still looks presentable.

I exit the bathroom and run into this girl. She had bright pink hair and was wearing a sexy black dress that formed to her curves perfectly.

"Oh, I'm sorry."

"It's fine. No blood, no foul." She smiles with perfect white teeth at me. Felix finds me again and asks if I want to dance. I agree and he pulls me into the gathering of other couples.

He placed one hand on my waist and held my hand with his other hand. I put one hand on his shoulder and let him hold my other hand.

He leads me around the ballroom and spins me around and lifts me into the air by my waist. The dance was fun and distracted me from my overwhelming thoughts.

Suddenly William cuts in and grabs my hand.

"May I?" Felix nods and I take William's hand. "I don't think I've ever seen my son look at someone the way he looks at you." He leans in really close to my neck.

"You know you smell absolutely divine."

I lean away from him and say, "Don't let the smell fool you. The angel blood only affects the smell. My blood still tastes like demon blood AKA hot garbage." He leans away from me and leads me back to Felix and his wife. Victoria reaches out to me and says she wants to talk.

We walk outside onto a balcony covered in blood red roses. Victoria leans to me. "You know before we met you, we were worried about our son dating someone who wasn't like us, but you are a real charmer. I think you'll be a great part of our family." I smile and she brushes my hair off my shoulder.

"I hope you two stay as happy as you are now."

"Me too." She cups my face in her cold hands and smiles.

"Now let's go back inside before they think I ate you." I chuckle and follow her back into the grand house.

CHAPTER THIRTY

The gala finally ended around 4:00 a.m., and the car that brought me there takes me home as well. I immediately get into the shower and wash my hair and face. It feels good to be home and away from people.

I dry my hair with a towel and change into a pajama set that I got for my birthday one year. It was silky and black.

I climb into bed and fall asleep instantly.

I wake up around noon that Sunday. Clark knew I was out late so he let me sleep. The dress lies in a heap on the floor of my room. I'll need to return that to my mom. I climb out of bed and go to get breakfa—lunch. It's lunch time.

I get ramen and sit on the couch and watch the news to see if I need to help people. The news was boring, so I turned on *Kitchen Nightmares*.

Suddenly I hear a knock on my door. Standing there was Ari crying her eyes out. I usher her in and sit her on the couch.

"What's wrong Arianna?"

"My parents are missing. They're not at home and I called their office and the people there said they left around an hour ago. So I called them and they didn't answer. I'm freaking out."

I rub her shoulder and ask, "Can you bring me something of theirs? I'll do a locating spell and find them."

"I didn't bring anything. We could head to my place and grab something there."

I nod. "Let me change first and then we'll leave."

"Okay." She nods, sniffing and wiping her eyes with her sleeve.

I put on my black, ripped mom jeans, an old band tee, and throw my hair up in a messy bun.

"Alright. Let's go." I grab my purse and slide into my black converse.

Ari springs up from the couch and we head out. I check my purse to make sure I have my book.

We greet Steve and head off to Ari's large apartment. The subway for once wasn't crowded and we made it to her apartment in ten minutes. She unlocks the door and we walk into her parents' room.

I grab a watch of her father's and a purse that's her mother's and sit down on their bed. I pull out the book and start to cast the spell. The objects start to float towards the door. We follow it out the door and down the hallways and through the city.

The objects lead us to an abandoned warehouse. I tell Ari to stay outside while I take care of things. I quickly transform into Supernova and slowly walk into the warehouse. Inside there is a group of people surrounding a small boxing ring. In the boxing ring were people in business suits and office wear. They were being forced to fight each other. I sneak behind people and stand there waiting for people to notice.

"Hello there," I say in my best "Obi-Wan Kenobi" voice. Everyone turns to me and the people in the ring look relieved. The man closest to me tries to punch me, but I grab his fist in midair and bend it backwards, hearing the bones crack and pop. The man screams and falls to the floor.

I grab another man who comes running at me. I swing the man by one arm and leg and whack the four men with the man.

The others start to grab weapons and attack me. I take them out quickly and bend a metal pipe around a guy's hand. The people seem to multiply by the minute. I keep fighting and fighting but more and more show up. A man takes a swing at my legs, but I fly up and hover just out of their reach. I fly down and slam my legs down on a group of men standing close together.

Finally I get through the last of the gang members. I jump into the ring and tell everyone they're free to go. Everyone thanked me and ran out. I smile and call Ari.

"I freed your parents. You should head home."

"Okay. Thank you so much."

"Of course." I hang up and fly home.

Clark was at home writing when I got there. He greets me and asks if I finished my homework. I told him I did, so I was going to just hang out around the apartment. He nods and goes back to writing.

CHAPTER THIRTY-ONE

I wake up on time for school today and am excited to see Felix. I eagerly hop out of bed and run to the bathroom. I brush my hair until it looks somewhat presentable. My hair cooperates and I pull it into a low bun at the base of my neck. I pull on a black and white striped long-sleeved shirt and a black skater skirt.

Clark had to leave early this morning, so I am alone today. I walk into the kitchen and make some eggs. They are good but not as good as Clark's.

I slide into my black Converse and grab my bag. The building has really become home to me over time. I love this place. I might even love it more than our old place.

The elevator here is so much better than our old place. I would sell my kidneys to never have to go on that other elevator in the morning ever again.

I say hello to Steve and rush to the train. Ivey meets me at the station and grabs my arm.

"I heard Ari's parents got kidnapped. Is it true?"

"Yes, but I saved them and all the others."

"Good. I hate seeing Ari sad."

"Me too." We walk onto the train and make it to school on time, thank God. I see Felix standing at the front of the school. He smiles at me and jogs over to me.

"Hey, how was your weekend?" he asks

"It was good. Tell your parents I had a good time and it was nice to meet them."

"I will." We walk to class, his arm around my shoulders.

Mr. Duke assigns us a group project and I have to work with Jessica. I would rather slam my tongue in a car door than work with her. But I suck it up and move over to a desk next to hers.

"So what book should we make this presentation about?" I ask.

"I don't know. You're the nerd, you figure it out."

I roll my eyes and start to think. "We could do *Pride and Prejudice*."

"Yeah, whatever, just do it." I kind of expected that I would be doing all the work and slapping Jessica's name on it. I choose the book and tell Mr. Duke and he tells us to head to the library. Jessica rolls her eyes and follows me out the door along with a few other pairs who have picked out their book.

Jessica spends the whole time we're at the library on her phone texting and on Instagram. I do all the research and check out the book from the library. The bell rings and we all disperse to our next class.

Lunch comes and goes and before I know it, the school day is over. I make it home and collapse onto my bed. Jessica was so awful today in class. I grab P&P from my bag and start reading it. The book is actually really good. I was having a good time. Clark knocks on my door a few hours later. I don't even realize I had been reading for hours. I finish the book in three hours. It was really good. I can't wait to do the project.

"Hey, Sky, I was worried when I didn't see you for a while, everything good?"

"Yeah, I just had a book to read for class and it kinda hooked me, so I finished it."

"Oh okay, Well, dinner's ready."

"Okay." I drag myself off my bed and follow Clark to the dining room. He puts a homemade taco in front of me and I devour it.

I finish dinner and head in to take a shower. The shower is short but nice and I change into pj's and crawl into bed. The best feeling is when my head hits the pillow. I fall asleep almost immediately.

CHAPTER THIRTY-TWO

The week goes by quickly and before I know it, it's Friday. I wake up with a letter on my pillow

Dear Darling Moondrop,

This Saturday evening there is a grand ball I wish you and your boyfriend to attend. I will help you find a dress and help you look the part of a princess. I do hope you agree to come. Please write yes or no at the bottom of this note and set it back on your pillow. If you say yes, I will grab you after school to help you prepare to be introduced to our court. I eagerly await your answer

Love,

Mom

I grab a phone off my bedside table and call Felix.

"Hello?"

"Hey, Felix, my mom just invited both of us to a ball tomorrow, would you like to come?"

"Sure, I'd love to meet your mom."

"Wonderful. I'll tell her we're coming. See you at school."

"See ya." I hang up and grab a pen from my bedside table. I scrawl yes on the bottom of the page and place the paper on my pillow.

I braid my hair back and pull on my black dress with the tortoiseshell buttons. I grab my long, gray cardigan and slide my hands through the sleeves. Clark yells at me to hurry up before my eggs get cold.

I run out of my room and scarf down my eggs. I'm running so late. I quickly text Ivey to go to school without me so she's not late. I slide into my Converse, grab my bag, and run out the door.

I actually make it to school on time somehow. I run to Mr. Duke's class and go to sit down next to Felix but Mr. Duke stops me.

"Everyone please sit with your partners." I groan and slump towards Jessica.

"So did you read the book or whatever?"

"Yeah I did. It was good." I pull out my laptop and I start on the presentation. Jessica just sits there on her phone. I wish Mr. Duke would look over and yell at Jessica to help me, but he just stares at his computer screen.

The bell rings and she did none of the work. I should probably tell Mr. Duke about it, but I don't want to piss her off even more than she already is.

I meet up with Felix before lunch.

"So, I guess I'll need something to wear tomorrow. Does a suit work?"

"I'll ask. But if not I'll find something for you."

"Thanks."

We walk through the line and head to our seat to find Ari crying. "What happened?" I ask.

"Reed cheated on me with Jessica." I look over at Jessica's table and see Reed sitting there with his arm around Jessica's shoulders. I hug Ari and try to cheer her up. Ivey stays by her side the entirety of lunch and even walks her to class. There's something about the way Ivey looks at Ari that raises some suspicion for me. I think Ivey might have a crush on Ari. I know Ari is pansexual, so she might like her back. They would look so cute together.

I walk to class with Felix and before he enters his classroom, he pulls me into a deep kiss.

"What was that for?"

"I just wanted to."

I smile and let him leave.

School ends quickly and I run home to see my mom and Clark sitting on the couch drinking coffee.

"Ahh, Mirnova dear, I'm so happy you and your boyfriend said you would come."

"Of course. Felix needs to know if he can just wear a suit or does he have to wear something special?"

"A suit is fine." I nod and text that to Felix. He replies with a thumbs-up emoji. I turn back to my mom. "Well, shall we go pick out a dress?"

"Yes, we shall," she says, rising gracefully off the couch and walks, almost floats, over to me. She grabs my hand and whispers a spell.

I open my eyes and see we're back in that grand bedroom from when I first borrowed a dress. My mom throws the closet doors open and starts picking out dresses she wants me to try on.

We start with an ugly purple and green ball gown with jewels on the bodice. A definite no. The next was a frilly pink thing with an A-line skirt with ruffles along it.

After literally fifty dresses, I try on this deep, royal purple with a large tulle skirt, off the shoulder straps and a sweetheart neckline.

"I love it."

"Me too." It fits me perfectly and makes me feel like a real princess. My mom walks into the closet and brings out a pair of sparkling black shoes. I told her no heels. I'm glad she found flats that work with the dress.

She opens a separate closet filled with tiaras and crowns. My mom seems to be skimming around, looking for a certain one.

"Ah, here it is," she exclaims. She picks up a black jeweled tiara with spike-like shapes rising from the base.

"It's beautiful. Can I really wear this?"

"Yes. Now that we have all that done, you should go get some sleep. I'll get you tomorrow to help you get ready. I'll also send someone to fetch your boyfriend."

"Thanks, Mom."

"Of course, Moondrop. Now, go to bed." She waves her hand in front of me and suddenly I'm back in my bedroom. I look at the time and see it's 10:00 at night. I quickly change into pajamas and climb into bed.

CHAPTER THIRTY-THREE

I wake up a little later than usual today. Clark already left for work, so I'm left to fend for myself. I make ramen (shocker, I know) and get comfy on the couch, waiting until it's time to meet up with my mom. The news was boring, so I don't need to help anyone. I turn on *Hotel Hell*, cause I finished *Kitchen Nightmares*. I love Gordon Ramsay.

I finish eating and washing my dish, but time is passing way too slow. I text Felix to remind him to be ready by seven as there will be someone there to pick him up. He thanks me.

I go into my room and look at my bookshelf. Maybe reading will help the time pass. I scan the shelf and pick out *Carrie* by Stephen King. I love this book, so I'm gonna read it again.

I plop on the couch and start reading. Thankfully it makes the time fly by and before I know it, my mom is tapping my shoulder, getting my attention. I turn to her and smile.

"Are you ready, Moondrop?"

"Yes."

She takes my hand and we're back in the bedroom instantly. She pulls me to a grand vanity and sits me in the chair in front of it. I go to pick up a hairbrush to start doing my hair, but my mom takes it out of my hand and says, "No, I am going to do your hair. I never got to when you were little, so this will make up for it."

"Okay." I settle into the chair and let my mom braid and twist my hair into a low bun with braids wrapped around it. I smile once she's finishes. It looks perfect.

Once my hair is done my mom helps me into my dress. She laces up the back and helps me into my shoes.

Finally, she places the tiara on my head and pins it to my hair so it won't fall off. It was surprisingly light.

"Alright, give me a twirl." I obey and slowly turn, my skirt flying out around me. It is beautiful.

"Your boyfriend is going to faint at how beautiful you look."

"Thanks, Mom."

"Now, I have to get ready." She sits at the vanity and starts brushing her long, black hair. It seems to magically form into perfect soft curls. She rises and grabs her dress out of the closet. It was white with gold branch-like lace covering it. The skirt was flowy and soft. I watch her pin a crown with large blue jewels to her hair. It is amazingly gorgeous.

She spins for me and asks, "How do I look?"

"Like a queen." She smiles and looks at the large clock on the wall.

"It's time." She takes my hand and leads me out of the room. She takes me through winding corridors until we make it to a grand set of double doors. The guards stationed at the side of each door open them when my mom signals them.

CHAPTER THIRTY-FOUR

The doors open to a grand ballroom. There are sparkling chandeliers hanging from the ceiling. The ceiling seems to be made of gold. The floor is made of polished marble. The grand staircase is decked out in gold and white roses. I am in awe at the sights in front of me.

At the bottom of the staircase is Felix in his fresh pressed suit. I smile as fanfare rings out and a person's deep and powerful voice rings across the ballroom.

"Presenting, Queen Irene Ellisite and her daughter, Princess Mirnova Tarteren." We descend the staircase and everyone bows for us. I let Felix take my arm once we make it to the bottom. My mom smiles at everyone. "Please, everyone, have a grand time." The band instantly picks up in a joyful tune. My mom turns to Felix and holds her hand out.

"You must be Felix. My daughter has told me a lot about you. She's quite smitten."

"As am I, Your Highness." He takes her hand and gives it a firm shake. He turns to me.

"Would you like to dance, Princess?"

"Do not ever call me that again, and sure." He lets go of my mom's hand and takes mine. We join the swirling bodies on the large main floor. It is magical. The chandeliers twinkle above us as he lifts me by the waist and watches the skirt of my dress poof out around us.

My eyes meet with my mother's and she smiles a huge smile at me. I smile back and focus again on Felix. The music swells and he does a fancy spin with me. I nearly fall, but he keeps a sturdy hand on my waist. I could feel other eyes on me and notice others whispering behind their hands. I tune in to one of the conversations someone was having.

"Did she really bring a filthy vampire to the ball? I can't believe someone like that will be our queen someday." My face falls and Felix notices.

"Are you alright, Sky?"

"Yeah, I'm fine. Let's just keep dancing." He nods and twirls me around.

We take a break from dancing so I can eat something. I walk over to the banquet table and pick at some sweets. They smelled like nothing I ever smelled before. One was fruity and smokey at the same time and another was chocolatey and sour. I try the chocolate one and it's surprisingly pleasant.

An older woman with dark skin and even darker freckles approaches me quietly.

"Your Highness?"

"Yes?"

"Hello, my name is Mara. I was the one who brought you to earth."

"Oh, well… hello. Thank you for getting me there safely."

"It was my pleasure." My mother comes rushing to my side.

"Come with me, Moondrop. I have some people to introduce you to." I nod and let her lead me to a man with large almost dragonfly-like wings sticking out of his back. A girl around my age with similar wings and a shimmering pink dress is standing with him.

"My dear Mirnova, this is Lord Jarniel Arimeyer, Lord of the fae and his daughter Miribella." Miribella reaches her hand out and I take it.

"It's lovely to meet you, Your Highness." I immediately recognize her voice as one of the people who was judging me for dating and bringing Felix here.

I smile a stiff smile and tell her it's nice to meet her as well.

Suddenly there is a loud bang from atop the grand staircase. There's a cloud of thick black smoke.

Once the smoke clears I see a man standing there. He has dark brown hair, deep set brown eyes, and a fancy set of armor on.

"I heard my niece was here." My mom suddenly appeared by my side.

"You and Felix get back to earth. Use this." She hands me a small flash bomb-like object. My mom turns back to the man and starts to talk rapidly in Elissite. I throw the object on the floor and in a puff of smoke Felix and I are in my bedroom.

It is cold in my room and I feel goose bumps appear on my arms. Felix shrugs out of his jacket and wraps it around my shoulders.

"Are you alright?"

"This was a huge night for my mom, and me and my uncle had to come and ruin it. I'm really mad. I want to go back and strangle him."

"An appropriate reaction." He grabs my hands and kisses them.

"Your mother made you come back to earth to keep you safe. I am not going to let you go back there and get hurt, okay?" I nod. "Now I want you to get changed into something comfortable and meet me in the living room so we can watch *Hotel Hell*."

"Okay." Felix rushes out of my room in a flash. He probably went to change his own clothes. I untie the bodice of my dress and slip the giant dress off. I take off the corset and put on some pajama shorts and one of Felix's hoodies that I stole. It is black and super soft.

I walk out into the living room and see Felix on the couch in pajamas, his arms open beckoning to me. I snuggle into him and turn on the TV.

CHAPTER THIRTY-FIVE

My mom told me I have to stay on earth for the time being until she can make sure I'll be safe from my uncle. I am sad, but I understand. It's hard not being able to see my mom or return the dress. That thing is just taking up all of my closet space. It's fucking huge. I now don't know why I chose this one.

Felix has been trying to make me feel better, but I'm still worried. Felix and I are cuddling on the couch watching TV when an emergency warning pops up.

With all the villains and other bad people attacking the city, the city has made an emergency alert for when they attack.

My head pops up and I start to get up.

"Be careful, babe," Felix says.

"Always am."

I change and fly out the window, heading towards downtown. When I get there, whole buildings have chunks of themselves missing. Standing in the middle of a plaza of broken buildings is a very tall black man with his arms motioning towards the buildings. Every time he motions his hand towards a building a whole piece of the building disintegrates into dust. Luckily, none of the buildings have fallen. I was ready to catch a building if it did fall. I know it's not practical to try and lift a whole building, but I don't care.

I slowly approach the man and try not to scare him. People are running in all directions and I'm glad the man is not dusting people.

"Oi, what the hell are you doing, dude?" I yell. The man's head snaps towards me.

"Ahh. The hero has arrived. Welcome, Princess. I am Laz." His eyes glow a deep red. He's a demon, and I just realize he spoke in Tarteren, the language of Tartarus. I try to answer him back in the same language.

"What are you doing here on earth? You're not supposed to be here."

"My king, Draven, told me to come here and look for you and your sister. It was dumb luck that you came to me. Now my king wishes to see you, won't you come with me, Princess?"

"Fuck no. Tell my uncle to eat my dick." I rush towards him with my staff raised. He tries to dust me, but he can't and I *thwack* him in the stomach with my staff. He doubles over in pain and I smirk.

"My uncle should've sent someone stronger."

He growls at me and tries to scratch at me, but I dodge him. I fly up higher and he aims his "dusting" hand right at me. He tries to hurt me but nothing happens. I smirk and I fly down and *whack* him in the head with my staff. He cries out in anger and tries to grab me out of the sky.

"Go back to hell where you came from!" I yell. He smirks and disappears in a cloud of thick black smoke.

I try a reverse spell on the destroyed buildings and watch them reform as if nothing happened to them. I smile contentedly and fly back home.

Felix is waiting there with open arms.

"I saw on the news. You did great. My girlfriend is a badass!" He raises his fist in victory. I smile and change back into my pj's. Felix beckons me to his arms and I snuggle into him. He smells heavenly. like old spice and rain. I love the way he smells. If I could bottle it I would.

Clark walks in a few hours later and smiles at us, still buried under blankets and arms wrapped around each other.

"You two look cozy."

"We are," I say.

Clark enters the kitchen and starts to make dinner for him and me. I smell pizza. The frozen kind, but pizza is pizza.

The pizza is good and it is kind of funny watching Felix sit awkwardly at the table while the two of us eat. I love the face he makes when he smells the pizza. It looks like someone dumped rotten garbage next to him.

"How can people eat food like that?"

"I don't know. How can you drink blood?"

"Touché." We all laugh and finish our dinner.

Dinner is good and Felix goes home.

CHAPTER THIRTY-SIX

I hate not knowing what's going on with my mom and my uncle. I hate him and am tempted to go find him and defeat him myself. Even Felix's attempts to comfort me have stopped working. I'm just so mad at Draven. I want him dead so my family can be together again. Once we find my sister, of course.

I drag myself out of bed and get ready for school. I pull on my ripped, black mom jeans and a NASA T-shirt. I throw my hair up in a messy bun and head out to breakfast.

Breakfast was normal and the trip to school was boring. When I get home, I see my mom standing in the living room. I run, throw my backpack down, and tackle hug her. We almost fall over, but my mom steadies herself on her feet.

"Mom! Is everything okay? Did you handle the whole Draven thing? Is it safe to be with you up in Elissium?"

"Slow down, Moondrop. Everything's okay. Your uncle has not been seen for weeks. We heard that he's been sending demons to try and take you to him. I'm glad you're safe. I'm here to let you know that I'm sending some angels down here to earth to protect you.

"You know I can protect myself. I'm a superhero. I've saved many lives."

"Really? Awww, I'm so proud! Well, I'm still going to have the angels sent here, but I will tell them to work out a signal for you to use if you need their help."

"That sounds good."

"Alright, Moondrop, I have to get back to take care of some things. I'll see you soon."

"See ya, Mom." She suddenly vanishes in a puff of white smoke and gold glitter. Some of the glitter gets in my mouth and makes me go into a coughing fit. I pat my chest with my fist and wait until I stop choking.

I finally get the glitter out of my lungs and sit down on the couch. It's good to have an update at least, but I hate that my mom feels the need for someone to protect me. I'm probably stronger than those angels she's sending down to watch over me. But then again, it might be good to have some backup around in case I need it.

I start my homework, but my mind keeps wandering back to my conversation with my mom.

Suddenly, three people dressed in armor holding long silver swords appear in my living room. They all drop to one knee and place their right fist on their heart.

"Your Highness, we are here to protect you. We will follow you everywhere to make sure you stay safe!" the biggest one, with buzzed-off brown hair and dark olive skin, basically shouts out at me.

I tell them all to stand up and ask, "Wait, won't people find it suspicious if they see you three walking around 'protecting' me?"

The tall girl with ivory skin and white-blonde hair steps forward.

"The humans cannot see us. You, however, will be able to see us but try to ignore us so as to not confuse the humans." I nod and we continue talking about important things like a movement I can do to signal that I need their help. The whole thing took about an hour and by the end of it, they all took up positions around the apartment to keep danger away.

I walk into my room, happy that none of my new bodyguards are inside. At least I get some privacy. I feel like the president right now. It's kind of annoying. I wish my uncle wasn't such a douchebag.

I finish my homework and walk out to the living room and see my bodyguards standing there at attention, their legs and arms stiff. Suddenly my phone chimes. My bodyguards all pull out their swords and go into an attack stance.

"Whoa, whoa. Calm down. It's just my phone. It's probably my brother or boyfriend." They all relax and go back into their stiff stance. I pull out my phone and see it's Clark. He says he's going to be in the office late, so I'm on my own for dinner.

"Well, looks like we're on our own for dinner." The angels don't move. I look away and whisper, "Okay." I walk into the kitchen and make a simple turkey sandwich. It's not the best dinner, but it's all I've got energy for. I sit on the couch and try to ignore the angels. This is going to take a while to get used to.

The sandwich is okay but really dry as we have no mayo. I text Clark to pick some up with the groceries this week.

Once I finish eating and finish my homework, I collapse into bed and fall asleep after warning my new guards about my brother coming home and telling them not to attack him.

CHAPTER THIRTY-SEVEN

School with my new guards is *sooo* weird. I can't stop looking over at them as they walk in a special formation. They keep telling me to stop looking at them and just go on with my day, but that's kinda hard when they draw their swords and threaten Felix for kissing me in front of the school. I hate this already.

Luckily, I have another shitty situation to deal with to distract me from the shitty guard one. I have to work with Jessica first period. I do all the work on my laptop, making the PowerPoint presentation look all nice and neat. It was all fancy and pretty and Jessica does none of it. She doesn't even look at the presentation, so I get an idea. At the end of the presentation, I tell the truth and give myself all the credit.

Lunch was even weirder with my guards. Felix asks me why I keep looking at nothing. I tell him what happened. He nods and grabs my hand.

"Remember, it is temporary."

"Yeah." I look over at Ari and Ivey and Ivey has her arm around Ari.

"*Sooo*, when did this happen?" I ask.

"Last period," Ari answers.

"Awww, you guys are so cute together," Lily gushes. They blush and we continue to eat. We eat in comfortable silence until we hear an ear-splitting scream from across the lunchroom. The scream comes from Jessica. I look over and see Reed hunched over on the ground covering his face. I run over and look at him.

His face was morphing into that of a dog; his hands forming into thick paws. There's another scream and another boy on the floor is morphing into a wolf.

Slowly but surely all the boys start becoming wolves. Oddly enough none of the girls are turning into wolves. I think it might be the food. I sniff the food Reed ate and it reeks of magic. Someone poisoned our food, but it only seems to affect men. I turn to my friends and we all share a look.

"Sky, go get the nurse or the principal," Ari says. I nod and run off towards the front office. I stop and slide into a vacant bathroom and hear my phone ring.

"Hello, we need Supernova right away at Thomas Jefferson High School. Someone poisoned our food and all the boys are turning into wolves."

"Alright, I'll contact her right away." I put my phone away and wait a few minutes after I yell for the principal and then transform. I run back to the commons and look at all the wolves running around running into things and sniffing each other and the girls.

"So, can someone tell me what happened?" I ask.

"I can." A booming voice comes from the kitchen. Out walks a man dressed in all black with clinking silver chains all over his pants.

"I was told to get you out in the open Miss Mirnova and convince you to come meet your uncle."

"I only want to see that man at my feet, with his blood on my knuckles, my foot on his chest and my sword at his throat."

"Then I guess these boys will stay wolves forever. You made your choice. I'll leave you to figure out how to reverse my spell. Ciao." He disappears in a puff of black smoke.

I turn back to everyone.

"I'll find a way to fix this. Don't panic." I pull out my book and look for curse reverse spells. I found a collection of twelve. My bodyguards stand in an alert stance and poke the wolves who get too close, confusing the hell out of them.

I try the first and easiest spell. The girls help me gather all the boys and keep them in one area. We flip tables over to build a barrier to keep them in.

I open my book and hold out my hand. I try the first seven with no results. I try two more and nothing. I look at the next one and see that it's a potion. That might work.

"Alright, girls, I need you to help me find these ingredients to try and reverse this spell. I need you to find salt, water, roses, clove, and vanilla. Find those things for me and meet back here.

After about ten minutes of hanging out with the dogs, which is actually not that bad. Maybe we don't have to change them back. I'm kidding. Or am I?

No, I am.

Finally the girls come back with the ingredients and hand them to me.

"Does anyone know where a bowl or pot is?"

"I'll go to the kitchen and grab one," Jessica says. For once she's thinking of someone other than herself. I'm kinda proud of her.

Jessica returns with a pot and I start to dump the ingredients in the pot and say the spell correctly. It starts to glow and bubble and turn a pale purple color. I throw the last rose petal in and the potion glows a bright gold color.

"Okay, it says we have to pour the potion on their heads so grab a cup and get started. One by one the boys turn back to humans as we pour the potion over their heads. The boys shake their hair and stand up, rolling and stretching their joints.

Once everyone is back to normal, I leave. I went home telling my friends to tell people the food made me sick.

I pull my laptop onto my lap (go figure) and log into Instagram. I scroll through the adoption tag until I find her. A girl with bright white hair and icy blue eyes who looks exactly like me down to the freckles that dot our cheeks. The post was her with her adoptive parents celebrating her "gotcha" day last year.

I immediately follow her and message her.

I type:

S: *Hello, my name is Skylar. I think you're my long-lost twin sister. I know that sounds crazy and I tried to think of a way to tell you this lightly and ease into it, but I have to be blunt. You might be my twin sister Nashmire.*

T: *Ummm Hi, I'm Tori. This does sound super weird, but I looked through your posts and noticed how we look exactly the same and we have the same "gotcha" day. Did your parents find you in a bush too?*

S: *A field actually. In the middle of Kansas.*

T: *Nice. Now is there a reason you contacted me? Besides to make me question my entire existence?*

S: *Our uncle is trying to capture us and use our special powers to take over the whole universe and I need your help to stop him.*

T: *Who's our birth mother? How did you know I have powers?*

S: *I have powers too and our mother is Queen Irene of Elissium and Tartarus.*

T: *You're pranking me.*

S: *I promise you I'm not. We need to get together. We are in immense danger when we're apart. How fast can you make it to New York City?*

T: *We're really in danger?*

S: *Yes and a lot of it.*

T: *Alright. Could you use your powers to come to me cause I'm in California and cannot afford a plane ticket?*

S: *Yeah hold on.*

I look at her Instagram and focus hard on her photos of her bedroom. I whisper the transportation spell and feel my body turn to smoke. Once I feel solid again I open my eyes and see my sister sitting on a large pink and black plush bed with baby pink walls behind her.

"Oh my God, that actually worked! I've never done that spell before." I turn to Tori. "Hi, I'm your sister, Skylar."

"Hi. I still need to pack some clothes and tell my parents."

"Before you do that, I have something for you." I pull out a small box and hand it to her. She gently takes it from my hand and our skin lightly touches.

"Jesus, your hands are cold!" I exclaim.

"Maybe your hands are just hot." She quickly opens the box and pulls out the necklace with a sun pendant.

"It's meant to match mine." She puts it on and looks at my moon necklace.

"Okay, time to tell my parents."

"Do you want me to come with you?"

"Yeah, that might make it easier. Come on." She grabs my arm and makes sure I'm behind her. We walk out into a cute, quaint living room with a gray couch and a soft-looking white blanket draped over top. We walk over to their small dining room where a man with fiery red hair and a beard sits with a stick-thin woman whose neck seems to go on for miles.

"Mom, Dad, something happened tonight and I have to go away for a bit."

The woman looks shocked. "What happened? Where are you going? You're only seventeen."

"I met my twin sister and now have an explanation of my strange powers. She's standing right behind me." At that moment I peek my head out from behind her and see the shock on their faces.

"We have to be together to be safe. I have to go with her to New York City. I'll be back once the danger has passed, but for the time being NYC is the safest place for me. Please understand."

"You're in danger? From what?"

I speak up. "Our uncle. He wants to use our powers to take over the universe. I'm going to take her with me to New York and contact our mother. Don't worry, I'll bring her back safely." They seem to think and then nod their heads.

"Be safe. We love you, Victoria."

"I love you too." She walks over and hugs them.

Tori drags me back to her room and I help her pack some clothes and toiletries. We don't know how long she's staying with me, so we pack as much as we can. We end up filling two giant suitcases and an extra bag with all of her shit. She says one last goodbye to her parents and we teleport back to my room. She has taken this shockingly well. I'm quite impressed.

CHAPTER THIRTY-EIGHT

To say Clark was surprised would be an understatement. When I showed him that Tori was here, he nearly fainted. I pulled out the extra air mattress we always keep in the closet and blew it up in my room. Luckily, I had extra sheets and blankets.

I help Tori unpack her stuff and put her clothes anywhere they fit. I let Tori take a shower to help her process what just happened. I still need to process what just happened. I lay on my bed and turn on some music.

After about twenty minutes, Tori returns in some pajamas she brought. They ar pink and silky. I invite her to sit on my bed.

"Do you want to meet our mom?"

"I would love to."

I whisper the spell and watch as our mother materializes in front of us.

"Hello, Moondr—is this…?"

"Yes. Hi, Mom, I think." Our mother throws her arms around Tori and squeals in joy. She motions to me to join the hug. I concede and wrap my arms around them both.

We stay together for almost five minutes until Mom breaks away.

"Now, we need to get you girls somewhere safe. Our double agent has discovered that Draven plans on attacking us in the next couple of days. My guess is he's going to start on earth with you two and try to get you to join him. The castle should be safe enough."

"No. I want to fight. If Draven is trying to take my future throne I want to fight to keep it. Let me don some armor and fight for my kingdom. I won't go down without a fight."

I stare my mother in the eye. She tries to challenge me in her gaze, but I hold strong.

"I want to fight too," Tori says.

"Alright, but you two must learn to fight as one. I know a spell that will combine you two together and let you fight as one all-powerful being. You two will have to work together. If you do, we can't lose." We both smile and grab our mother's hands so she can take us to the castle of Elissium.

Instead of the large, grand bedroom I was used to seeing, we appeared in some sort of training room. Our mom disappears for a split second before returning with a large old-looking book. She makes the book float in front of her and flips through the pages before stopping on one piece.

"Here we are. Alright, are you two ready?"

"I know we just met, but I trust you, and that doesn't normally happen, so...," Tori says, grabbing my hand. Mom says the spell and I feel my body become almost liquid. My bones become putty and my muscles become viscous. I feel my body combined with Tori's until we are one being.

I move our hand and stretch our fingers in front of our face. Our nails have turned black and sharpened to a deadly point. Our hair falls down our shoulders in a mix of purple and white hues. Tori moves our other hand and pulls at a chunk of our hair.

"I think it worked." Our voice came out doubled.

"Wonderful. Now, we must at least give you basic combat training if we are going to do this. Now, I want you two to work together and punch this bag as hard as you can."

We walk sort of awkwardly up to the punching bag and try to swing our fist as hard as we can. We miss the bag entirely and keep missing it for three hours while we're in the training room. Finally we hit the bag dead center and watch it fly off the stand and burst open spraying small plastic beads everywhere.

"That was great, you guys. Just keep doing that. Now I want you to practice using your magic. Hit this dummy with a fireball." She pulls over a tall black dummy on a stand. It only takes us thirty minutes to get used to using our powers while we're combined. I'm highly proud of myself and my sister. We're really starting to get the hang of this. Walking is still kind of hard, but we're making do.

Once training is done, Mom still wants us to stay together for one more thing. She takes our hand and leads us to the armory. She shows us to a small corner of the room. Inside there is a chest full of armor pieces that look like they will fit us. Mom starts digging around in the chest and pulling out pieces and holding them up to our body, shaking her head, and pulling out a different piece.

She finally settles on a set of shiny black armor that looks like it will fit us like a glove.

"Okay, we have to see if this works." She helps us put on the armor pieces. We strap the chest plate over our flat chest and did up the buckles. I was right, it fits us like a glove.

We pull on the arm pieces next and fasten them around our biceps and wrists. Next came the leg pieces and our mom helps us into them.

The armor clunks loudly as we walk around the room getting a feel for it.

"I think this will work," we say. Mom smiles and helps us out of it.

"Alright, let's split you two up again." We nod. Mom chants the proper reverse spell and I feel my body liquify again. I feel like a cell going through mitosis.

Once we're apart, I flex my hands and arms and stretch out.

"Oh it feels good to have my own body back," Tori says, hugging herself. I agree wholeheartedly.

CHAPTER THIRTY-NINE

Mother had some of her ladies maids show us to a giant room with two king-sized beds and tall painted walls. The ceiling and walls were painted to look like the night sky. The stars seemed to glow as if they were actual balls of gas floating millions of miles away from us in a different part of the vast universe.

I run my hand over the bed I chose. The sheets are silky and soft. Both beds are adorned with a fuck ton of throw pillows.

I flop down onto the bed and smile.

"You look happy. I have a question," Tori says.

"Shoot."

"Were you and Iren—I mean Mom really looking all over the world for me. Am I really that special?"

"Have you not used your powers in day-to-day life?"

"No, my parents thought my powers were a curse."

"Well, they're wrong. Yes, Mom was looking all over the world for you, and yes, you really are that special. Come let's do a sister thing. Let me braid your hair." I motion her to sit on my bed. She smiles and runs over, plopping down in front of me. I take her long, shiny, white hair that smells faintly of strawberries and start to twist and braid it into a complex pattern on her head.

It was two hours until I was done. We talked the whole time. We talked about so many things, just getting to know each other. She's a really fun person.

Once I finished, I lead Tor—Nashmire over to the vanity against the wall between two windows. She admires what I did with her hair and envelops me in a hug.

"This was fun. We should do this all the time."

"I agree. Now let's get to sleep just in case the battle is tomorrow and we have to be ready." She nods and starts to take her hair out of the braid.

We open the closet and find a plethora of clothes of many different styles.

We have to look for a good five minutes before we find the pajamas. Nash grabs a pale cream nightgown and I pick a black nightgown that goes down to my knees.

We change and climb into bed. The bed is *sooo* comfortable. I never want to leave it. I sink into a restful sleep in no time.

Nash wakes me up and tells me that Mom wants us to dress in battle clothes just in case and to find something in the closet again. I nod and climb out of heaven, oops—I mean bed. I pull on some tight black pants and a loose gray shirt. I also pull on some brown knee high lace-up boots. Nash is wearing some gray pants, a white short-sleeved shirt and some short black boots.

We get really lost looking for the dining room but finally find a maid to ask and she graciously leads us there. Sitting at a large, glossy wooden table is our mom dressed in, for the first time that I've ever seen, in black pants, a blue and black tunic with a hood, and some thigh-high black boots. I sit down next to her and across from Nash and dig in. The food is cooked to perfection. I basically stuff my face. It is so good. Nash seems to agree and we both eat seconds.

After breakfast we head to the training room and combine once again. This time we train in our armor. It is hard at first, but we get used to it. We use our unique powers to help each other fight better as one. I use my super strength to lift our limbs in the armor where Nash uses her better reflexes to move our limbs faster. We combine my heat and her cold and form a strong beam of power we can attempt to blast out of our hands. It's really hard and we keep failing, but we keep trying and trying. We finally get a little ball of energy to form in our hand but it fades as quickly as it appears.

"Dammit!" we yell at our failure.

"It's okay, you'll get this." Mom rubs our shoulder.

We try again. We place our hands together and slowly open them focusing on our power flowing through our hands. Finally, we see a beam of blue magic shoot out of our hands and obliterates the dummy. We jump for joy, our armor clanging and clacking as we jump. Our mom envelopes us in a hug, the fucking armor made it a little awkward.

Suddenly there's a loud boom from the east side of the castle. Mom grabs our hand and teleports us to the armory where she quickly puts on her silver set and grabs two swords and hands one to us.

"How are we supposed to use this thing?" Nash asks in our voice. I talk to her out loud.

"I've fought before so just follow my lead." She nods our head and we follow our mom to the site of the boom. There is a gaping hole in the side of the castle wall and demons are crawling in from every direction chasing and grabbing at and all around harming people. I summon our wings, they are a mixture of white and black. Mom follows us and I pull out our sword.

We fight demons of all shapes and sizes until I feel a familiar presence. Walking down the path, splitting the horde of demons like Moses split the Red Sea is Olivar. Alive. Well alive-ish. His eyes are glowing a sinister red color and he has black veins snaking up his face. I run towards him despite Nash's interference. I look at his new, demonic face and nearly start crying. Finally, Nash gets my attention and tells me to look who's behind Olivar. It's Draven.

I almost get close enough to touch Olivar when he pulls out a demon glass sword and runs toward us. I block his first attack and feel an ache in my heart as Nash takes over to fight. I want to cry. Draven took someone I loved and turned him into a monster. He is not my Olivar. I try to help fight, but I feel like I just got punched in the gut fifty times. Nash finally gets him down but doesn't kill him. She must sense that I care about him. She just knocks him out.

We turn to Draven and try to blast him with our magic beam but nothing happens. For fucks sake, of course it decides not to work. We try again to no result. Draven laughs at us and grabs our wrist. Suddenly we're enveloped in a thick cloud of red smoke.

CHAPTER FORTY

The smoke clears and suddenly we're standing in a grand throne room, much like the one in mom's castle, but this one is different. This one is made of smooth black stones and has fiery torches lining the red carpeted path up to the spiky black throne. We are also split again, which is nice. I still had the sword in my hand as my uncle appears on the throne.

"Welcome, girls, to your new home. I do hope you like it here, but then again I really don't care about your feelings. You two are the best weapons of mass destruction and could help me finally take my rightful place on the throne of Elissium and Tartarus."

"We will never help you," I spit at him.

"Oh, but you will, if you want to keep your precious father safe."

"You have our father?" Nash yells. Draven turns to two guards in fancy helmets that look like they won't come off, standing at either side of the hallways behind the throne.

"I think my dear older brother would like to meet his precious daughters, don't you?" The guards nod and head off down a hallway.

The guards return after about five minutes. They return with a man in chains. The man has shoulder-length black hair and a long beard. The man is wearing scrappy clothes in an ugly brown color and he doesn't look us in the eye at first but once he feels our presence, he looks up and makes eye contact with me. I recognize those eyes. I see them every time I look in the mirror.

"Dad?" I ask. He tries to go and hug us, but the chains and guards stop him. Draven sees this desire and waves the guards away.

"No, no, let the man meet his children. I'm sure it's hurts him to be away from them for so long." The guards back off and our father slowly shuffles to us and wraps his arms around us.

"My girls! My little girls! Oh! How I missed you."

I speak to him in a whisper.

"We are going to get out of this. We just need to use our beam and Draven will be no more."

"Do it quickly." The guards suddenly drag him away from us and tells us that if we act up then our father will pay the price. I grab Nashmire's hand and whisper the combine spell. I still have the sword in my hand.

Draven sees us form together and laughs. "So that's how you want to play it." He pulls out his own sword and struts confidently over to us. He swings his sword at our head but Nash's reflexes help us dodge it easily. I swipe our sword with all my strength and slash him across the leg. Thick black blood oozes out of the long gash I left on his leg.

"Damn brats!" He swipes at our face and nicks us in the eyebrow. We slash him again, this time in the arm. He gets us in the arm and I feel her healing kick in and our wound closes quickly. The battle is intense. Draven gets us right in the temple. Thick black and silver blood drips down our face and onto the floor. Our vision goes fuzzy and we sway on our feet for a single moment. He tries to use that time to get us, but Nash's reflexes kick in and we dodge his advance on us and he lets out a loud and angry grunt.

I swing and manage to cut a piece of his hair off the top of his head. He laughs as his hair falls to the floor. Draven swings at us again and gets us right in the armor. Now it's our turn to laugh. He roars angrily and charges us. We spin on our heel and manage to slash him in the leg. Nash moves our sword to cut him across the cheek as he's so close to us. I can smell the rancid smell of demon blood drip even more on the floor. I nearly gag, but I control myself and jump away from our uncle. He's panicking and clutching his leg.

"You little brats are stronger than I thought." He charges once more and slices us on our armor again. He seems really angry. He drops his sword and tackles us to the floor. He wraps his hands around our neck. We start to dig our pointed nails into his arms to get him to release us, but he just holds tighter. Luckily, I don't need air to live so…. He really should do more research on our powers. Finally, he realizes this is doing nothing and lets go. I snake my legs to where my feet will be on his shoulders and force him down so now I'm sitting on top of him. We start to pound our fists on his face, watching the thick black blood drip from his nose and seeing bruises forming already. Nash tries to stop, but I keep punching.

"Nova, stop. He's almost unconscious," Nash says in our mind.

I snap out of my rage and we summon our sword from across the grand hall and step on Draven's chest. We point the sword at his throat and go to deliver the final blow.

"No!" we hear our father cry out. "Don't kill him. He doesn't deserve that mercy." The guards, seeing the sight in front of them release our father and back off. Dad lets me break the chains around his wrists and melt them onto Draven's wrists. He screams from the heat and I revel in it. That's what you get for hurting my family.

The castle seemed to shake almost and suddenly, it was no longer black and dark and creepy but grand and gothic. The stone became a beautiful cream color with accents of black. Life seemed to return to the realm. We smile and hug and send the guards, who look so different now. They look happy and the helmets are gone. They had actual faces. We separate and summon our mom.

Mom appears in a puff of white smoke and looks around. Dad and her eyes meet and they run to each other and wrap their arms around each other. They kiss and Mom says Dad needs a haircut and to shave. He chuckles and motions for us to come join him. We all hug and teleport back to Elissium. My dad looks around and smiles even wider.

"Oh, I've missed this," he says as he sits on his and mom's bed.

"Me too," Mom says, joining him on the bed. Suddenly we hear a knock on the door. A guard walks in and says that there is a demon who wants to speak with me. I say I will, thinking I know who it is.

I step out into the hallway and see demon Olivar standing there.

"Hello, Sky."

"Hi, Olivar." He runs up to me and envelopes me in a hug. I pull away.

"Olivar, I can't be with you. I've moved on. I met someone else."

"That makes me so happy. I will leave you and your relationship alone. See ya." He waves and walks away. I smile and head back into the room.

We all share one more big hug and I pull away and say, "Well, this is amazing and all, but I have to get back to earth. I have a test tomorrow, and I think we should give you and Dad some alone time." Nash nods and Mom and Dad smile sadly.

"Alright. But one more hug and you must visit more. Especially, you

Mirnova, I have to help you learn to become a proper queen." We all hug and wave goodbye as we fade into purple and white smoke.

When I open my eyes, I'm back in my bedroom. My phone rings and I see it's from Felix. I answer.

"Hello."

"I heard about the battle. Are you okay? Did you win? Wait, obviously you won cause I wouldn't be talking to you if you'd lost."

"I'm fine, really. Also we saved my dad and now my uncle will rot in jail for the rest of time."

"Good, good. We should celebrate some time."

"I'd like that. Well, I am so tired after today, so I'm gonna go, good night. Love you."

"Good night, love you too." I practically run to the shower and wash away the dirt and blood off my person. Today is a day that people will talk about forever. I hop out of the shower and pull on Felix's hoodie and some shorts and go to sleep thinking about what tomorrow will bring for me. My life can be kind of crazy. But if you're reading this you probably already know that. Let's just see what life brings use.

Sleep well.

www.ingramcontent.com/pod-product-compliance
Lightning Source LLC
Chambersburg PA
CBHW070837160726

48004CB00001B/420